If the Broom Fits

SARAH SUTTON

IF THE BROOM FITS

For information, contact:

http://www.sarah-sutton.com

Cover Design © Designed with Grace

Image © DepositPhotos – golyak

First Edition: October 2020

10 9 8 7 6 5 4 3 2

ALSO BY SARAH SUTTON

LOVE IN FENTON COUNTY:

WHAT ARE FRIENDS FOR
OUT OF MY LEAGUE
IF THE BROOM FITS
CAN'T CATCH MY BREATH
TWO KINDS OF US

To all my fellow ghosts and ghouls

One

Kids were cute and all, but so flipping *loud*. Especially around sugar cookies and an inflatable bounce house.

Two little fairies with purple wings fluttered past me while doing that laugh-scream thing kids did, making a beeline for the bouncy castle that took up so much real estate in the backyard. A dragon, a mermaid, and a robot were hot on the fairies' heels, chasing them to the plastic deathtrap. The robot's pipe-cleaner antennas flapped around as the boy hurried along to catch up, his cardboard head bumping with the movement.

I shouldn't have been judging his costume. My costume wasn't so spectacular, either. In fact, it really, really itched, and I felt really, really stupid. The sheer sleeves didn't mix well with the October air. Goosebumps freckled my skin, and I had to fight the urge to cross my arms.

"Princesses are supposed to *smile*, Blaire Beverly."

Being told to smile made me want to do the opposite,

especially when someone used my full name. I turned to find who'd spoken. "Then why aren't *you* smiling, Gram?"

My grandmother swatted at me with her free hand, perfectly balancing the tray of orange refreshments in the other. She'd woven her graying dark hair into an intricate braid, tied into a knot at the base of her neck, though a few strands escaped. "I've got enough wrinkles for you to know that I smile. Can you *try* to be cheerier?"

Cheeriness felt a little more than elusive at this point, and she shouldn't have been talking. She got to wear *pants* —I had to wear a blue-and-white dress that made me feel more like an imposter than a princess. The corset wrapped around my ribs made it hard to breathe, let alone be cheery.

I forced my lips to stretch to prove my less-than-authentic merriment, but the sticky lip gloss made me cringe. "How can anyone be cheery in these shoes? Did you have to get actual glass slippers, Gram?"

Gram rolled her eyes at me. "It isn't my fault you picked heels that are too small."

Fine, I *had* picked the shoes that were a size too small for my feet. On accident. And maybe they weren't *actually* made of glass, but something pretty dang close. Something equally torturous. I'd officially lost feeling in my toes an hour ago.

"Where's your tray?" Gram finally took note of my empty hands. "You're supposed to be serving the bacon-wrapped pieces of ham. Mrs. Wilson wanted those passed out for the kids, remember?"

I looked down at my hands, at the lines of black that

still edged around my nails. Gram had made me scrub off my polish on the way over here, which had been a feat in the tiny catering truck, but a few traces still remained. "Donnie went to get another one for me."

Gram raised one of her silvery eyebrows, and though she meant to be scolding, she couldn't totally eclipse the sliver of amusement. "You gave him your shoe sob story too, didn't you?"

I feigned indifference. "Does it matter?"

"Princesses are selfless, Blaire." She readjusted her grip on the tray, careful not to spill a drop of liquid as she walked away.

"I'm not a princess," I called after her. Quite frankly, I never wanted to hear the word *princess* again. See, Gram loved this kind of thing—parties, people, mingling. She lived for moments like this and couldn't wait to fill her day planner with costume parties.

Oh, and Gram loved Halloween. Whereas, me? I *hated* it. Vehemently. Passionately.

Don't get me started.

Gram owned a catering business called Costumed Catering. It'd been her baby for nearly three years, and in a tight community like ours, it thrived. Especially in October, because no town loved Halloween more than the Village of Hallow. *No*, they hadn't named the village after the holiday, but one might've thought so with how insane everyone got around this time of year.

And by insane, I meant *crazy*. We'd done ten costume

parties so far this month, and it was only the seventeenth of October.

And at how many of those parties had I been a princess? Ding, ding, ding—all ten of them.

The sheer veils attached to my sleeves caught in the wind, billowing behind me. One might think after all the times I'd been forced to play this princess role, I'd have gotten good at it. Good at faking that smile, at wearing the heels from hell. Honestly, I doubt I'd have much of a problem with dressing up if I got to be something cool, like a witch or a ghost.

But no, I had to be a pretty, pretty princess. *Ugh.*

"One tray of hors d'oeuvres for the lady," a light voice said, and a silver platter appeared at my right, full of crescent rolls and mini hot dogs. "Now, don't eat all of them this time or Gram's going to figure it out."

Freckle-faced Donnie and I made up the crew of Gram's Costume Catering business, or at least we were the face. My step-uncle, John, manned the truck parked on the street, making more trays of food whenever we needed them. John had married my dad's sister, Aunt Aimee, when Donnie and I were in the eighth grade, officially implanting both him and Donnie into this crazy, partially messed up family. Though the messed up side only affected my life.

There used to be one other honorary member of Costume Catering, but I pushed that thought from my head.

"Thanks," I said, taking the tray from Donnie. He wore a costume too, fully decked out as a pirate. He even had a parrot, one he'd duct-taped to his puffy shoulder pad. He'd gelled his black hair up into wild spikes, and though one would assume he designed it like that for his costume, he actually loved wearing his hair crazy. "I'll tell her a bunch of the little demons jumped me and devoured them all."

"Lower your voice," Donnie murmured quickly, glancing around at whoever stood closest to us. "One of the big demons will hear you and chew you out for it."

"These moms don't scare me," I told him, spotting where the majority of them stood near the "punch" table. Their costumes were almost nicer than their kids', as if more time had been spent on them than the fairy's and the robot's. "Besides, they're already on their fifth round of mimosas—they probably don't even know which kid is theirs."

Donnie took a large step away from me, as if he could distance himself from my words. "You need a censor. Someone to go around and go '*beep*' to cut you off. I'm surprised Gram still lets you on the front side of things."

That made me smile, but I tried to keep it small as I looked down at him. "I think you're finally starting to uncover my evil plan, Donnie."

He reached up and pressed his fingers to his lips, something he did frequently when he grew nervous. His parrot wobbled with the movement, almost falling off. "Your plan of, what? Offending the entire population of Hallow? I mean, you've already offended about half already, right?"

"I would've said three-quarters." I glanced down at the silver tray. If I angled it just right, my reflection gazed back at me, a whole lot of blonde and blue and chiffon. "I'm not *trying* to hurt people's feelings. It just, you know, *happens*. People can be crybabies."

"Who's a crybaby?" asked a little girl at my feet, stopping at my words. She was dressed like a scarecrow, and her blue eyes were wide as she watched me. I would've guessed she was four or five, but all short kids looked the same to me. "My brother calls me a crybaby, but I'm not one," she said, tone wobbling as her lower lip popped out. "I'm a big girl."

"You *are* a big girl." I passed my tray off to Donnie, who gave me a look that said *don't crush her dreams, please*. Ignoring him, I bent down in front of the little scarecrow. Her red plaid shirt went down way past her fingers, so I pushed the material up and out of the way so I could hold her hands. "Definitely not a crybaby," I told her with the gentlest voice I could muster. "Bigger than me, I'd say."

"But you're really big." Her eyes went to Donnie, who clutched the tray nervously. "You're bigger than him."

I nearly snorted. "You're right, I am tall. But just because I'm tall doesn't mean you're not bigger than me." I gave a little gasp. "I have an idea. I can use my magic and make you a super-big girl."

The little girl didn't look impressed. "Princesses don't have magic."

This time, I did snort. "I'm a special kind of princess, one with magical powers." I dropped my voice, looking at her drawn-on freckles and straw woven through her hair. "You have to close your eyes."

After a moment of deciding whether or not to trust me, she pinched her eyes shut. "Will it hurt?"

"Of course not." I placed both of my hands on either side of her head, the straw in her hair bending under my touch. Wiggling my fingers, I tapped magic against her skull, all over. Her forehead, her temples, on the crown of her hair. After a second, I pulled back. "It worked!"

Stubby baby teeth greeted me when the little girl grinned, mega-bright and excited. She pressed her tiny hands over her head, eyes round. "I feel it! I'm so much bigger! I got to tell Daddy!" She hurried off in the direction of the moms and dads, her run a little uneven with her hands on her head.

I rose to my feet, wincing as the shoes bit into my squished toes.

"See," Donnie muttered, and handed me back the tray, "why are you so nice to kids? You go all 'ooh, magic, ooh' on them, and it wins them over. I thought kids annoyed you."

"You can still be annoyed by someone and still love them." I glanced at him. "I love you, don't I?"

Donnie gave me an unamused glare.

"Kids still have all their hopes and dreams," I said, watching as the scarecrow nudged the leg of a man in dark navy scrubs, a man who hadn't turned from laughing with his friends. "Those dreams are perfect. I don't want to be the one to crush them."

I knew a thing or two about crushed dreams, especially when it came to family. A pinching sensation took home in my heart the longer I watched the little girl trying to gather the attention of her father, the longer he continued to ignore her.

The pain became so sharp that it nearly knocked all the air from my lungs. "Come on," I told Donnie, pulling my gaze away. "These things won't serve themselves."

two

The August before I'd started high school, my mother had passed away. It'd been from a freak thing—a virus that had attacked her immune system—and it'd taken her quickly. So quickly that I hadn't had time to fully wrap my brain around the fact that she'd been sick. Neither Dad nor I saw it coming.

My dad, though, had taken it worse. He'd gone from a great dad to a barely functioning human being. The absence of Mom's light from our lives had thrown us into total darkness, and we couldn't find the end of the tunnel.

Until Gram had stepped in. She came over and made sure we'd gotten up for the day, helped us cook dinner, taken me back-to-school shopping. For almost two months, things had been okay. Dad and I had learned how to somewhat function together again with a little piece missing. It'd still been hard—hard to crack jokes Mom would've laughed at, hard to acknowledge that the space she filled in our lives would always be empty.

Even though it'd been painful, I'd thought things would be okay. Time heals all wounds, as they said.

Until, late in the night on October 30th two years ago, Dad left. Left Hallow and left me behind.

And now, two years later, I stared at the front of my ugly orange locker door, thinking *good riddance.*

I kicked the corner of the door, popping the hinge that liked to stick shut, and getting a good glimpse into my mess of a space.

It served as a catch-all for crap. Everyone else had those organizing things for their lockers, or the metal shelves to keep their books off the floor, but I didn't. I thrived in this self-made disorder.

I'd crammed three jackets inside, two of which were crumpled on the bottom underneath textbooks and old homework worksheets. I'd used a galaxy-themed tape to stick magazine clippings to the metal sides, their corners peeling after only a month of hanging.

Chaotic. Just as I liked it.

"A double chocolate espresso for my favorite girl," Donnie announced as he came up to my locker, offering a teal-colored coffee cup. The logo from our favorite coffee shop, Crushed Beanz, glared in black script on the side. "I may or may not have had a sip. And then died a little inside as my soul shriveled to dust."

"That's because you're used to the frou-frou of pumpkin spice," I told him, hanging my backpack on one of the hooks and taking the cup. The scent of coffee hit my nose, eliciting a shiver down my spine. "Soul-crushing coffee is my favorite."

"Makes sense." Donnie brought his own cup to his lips and sipped, loudly. His denim jacket swamped him, a few sizes too big, and he had to roll the sleeves up to expose his hands. The gel in his hair shined under the hallway lights. "You're lucky I drive past Crushed Beanz on my way into school."

I couldn't help but agree with him on that. Coffee before school was a tradition, started last fall, and the idea of giving up that caffeine boost before school made me want to cry.

Only, Donnie never used to get the coffee before school. No, that job had belonged to someone else.

I took a long drink from my espresso, heat filling my mouth. I would need the buzz to survive today—or at least survive until lunch. And I had to drink it fast. Mr. Miller— our first period teacher—didn't allow outside drinks into his classroom. No coffee. The monster.

"Incoming," Donnie said under his breath, and my body locked up at his tone, heart stopping before jump-starting at full speed.

I turned and faced the inside of my locker, gaze tracing where screws kept it fastened together, where my galaxy tape began to peel, where my backpack hung on a crooked hook. If I looked at all these things for the next few minutes, I'd be fine. The moment would pass. I couldn't turn and look. I couldn't turn and...

I looked.

I couldn't deny the compulsion, a familiarity that two weeks couldn't erase. So, yeah, I lifted my chin and peeked over my shoulder, uncaring of the consequences.

Hallow divided its love between two things—Halloween and high school football. Our school's team wasn't anything too stellar, but last year when they'd made the playoffs, the entire community had rallied. I could still remember the excitement behind that final game, and even though we'd lost, the celebration had lasted nearly a week.

Seeing a few guys from the football team walk down the hallway now, though, didn't elicit nearly the same amount of excitement. Not until I saw who spearheaded the pack.

Once upon a time, I'd fallen in love with a boy named Lucas Avery, and things had been perfect. He was the kind of guy who would order extra French fries and let me steal some from his plate. The kind of guy who'd bring me chicken soup when I didn't feel good, without even being asked. The kind of guy who'd known my coffee order by heart. His eyes would crinkle at the corners, his left cheek would dimple ever so slightly, and his mouth—oh, his mouth—would curl into this smile that left my knees weak. Heartthrob Lucas Avery, a dream come true.

Once upon a time, we'd been happy.

Until I shattered that dream like glass.

Lucas walked down the hall now with his friends in tow as if in slow motion, a blue T-shirt hugging his shoulders, worn denim jeans cuffed at the ankles. He used to keep his espresso-colored hair cropped, barely long enough to run my fingers through. Now, it swept a little into his eyes as he walked, and I knew without looking that those eyes were blue. Dark, dark blue.

And, out of habit, Lucas's gaze slid effortlessly to mine. One, two, three seconds ticked by before I came to my senses, turning back to my locker. A curl of pain started to unfold in my chest, a longing I couldn't easily shove down. *Don't come over here, don't come over here, don't come—*

"Hey, you two," a familiar voice said, tone so low that the words caressed my ears, tickled down my spine. I focused on my locker, trying to ignore the internal reaction. "How's the coffee this morning?"

"Mine's good," Donnie replied cheerfully. *Traitor.* "I ordered extra cinnamon this time, so it's really—" He glanced over at me and found me giving him a death stare. It made him freeze. "Uh, good. I see you stopped by Crushed Beanz too, huh?"

Lucas shifted in the corner of my vision, his teal cup catching my eye when he lifted it. "All those morning coffee runs left me addicted. I blame you, Blaire."

The way my name fell so effortlessly from his mouth had every inch of me twitching, as if electrocuted. *You were the one who started that coffee tradition,* I thought, pretending to carry on the conversation in my head. It made me feel a little better about not speaking to him aloud, like I *wasn't* ignoring him.

"Although, I'm not like you," he went on. "I couldn't drink that espresso nonsense—I actually like my taste buds."

I closed my eyes, glad for my curtain of blonde hair to shield my expression from him. *I know. You usually get a large hot caramel macchiato, two pumps of toffee nut flavoring, light on the espresso.*

The next time Lucas spoke, he lowered his voice, the soft tone a teasing whisper. "You really going to pretend I'm not here, Bee?"

It took everything in me not to shiver from the gravelly tone, to not respond. Especially because he'd used my nickname—the one only he used, a term of endearment more than a name itself. It still made butterflies flutter in my stomach, a muscle memory.

I focused on the back panel of my locker, on the small chip of orange paint near one of the screws, offering nothing but a tense silence.

This was the dance we moved to now—and I played it on repeat. Focusing on everything but Lucas Avery, waiting for him to turn away.

And, after a few moments of waiting hopelessly for my reply, he did. "Well, you two have a good morning," Lucas said easily, as if I hadn't full-out pretended he wasn't there. I could still feel those dark eyes, though, always lingering. "See you around, Donnie," he added, and headed off to join his buddies.

With him gone, all the oxygen poured back into my lungs.

I thought things would've gotten easier. That after a while, it would've been easier to be around him, to see him walking in the hallways, but it wasn't. Each and every time, it left me breathless. Disoriented. Aching.

"Are you ever going to tell me what happened between you two?" Donnie demanded, watching as I pulled my supplies from my backpack. I didn't know whether or not he could tell that my hands shook. "I mean, you were together for a year and a half, and two weeks ago, you dump him out of the blue? I'm your best friend, Blaire. You can tell me."

"Irreconcilable differences," I said blithely, bringing my cup to my lips. The answer came close enough to the truth that I could avoid a longer explanation, but I couldn't tell Donnie everything about our breakup. I wasn't sure he'd have understood my decision.

Heck, when I could smell Lucas's cologne, I wasn't sure I understood my decision either.

I downed my espresso in a few scalding gulps, slamming my locker door shut while noting the time. Three minutes until the bell. With a pat on Donnie's shoulder, I said, "Drink up, pumpkin boy, or Mr. Miller will dump your extra-cinnamon nonsense down the drain."

Gram and I lived in a three-bedroom apartment on Lagos Street, right in the center of all things *community*. Town-hall was four doors down, and right across the street was Hallow Square, the community park that held all the events, the Halloween Boo-Bash included. Even though I hadn't attended since Mom had died and Dad had left, I still had a front-row seat of that nonsense, my bedroom window overlooking it all.

The shop space directly downstairs from our apartment was the central hub to Costume Catering, where all the pre-baking and tray-arranging happened.

I clambered through the front door of the apartment, house keys jingling noisily. It had Gram's spare food truck key on it, though I was never allowed to drive it, as well as the key to the P.O. box. "Gram?" I called to the quiet house. "Are you up here or downstairs?"

"In the costume room," she returned, voice close.

Gram kept all the costumes and wigs and accessories in the extra bedroom in the apartment, giving us access to princess dresses and pirate hats 24/7. More often than not, I'd find her tucked between the clothing racks, doing some alteration or another. The crafty side of her couldn't help it —when she got in her head that she wanted to add lace or alter a neckline, it had to be done. And having the costume room upstairs was much easier than running back and forth every time inspiration struck.

When I walked into the narrow room, I found Gram sitting at her work desk, quickly flattening the princess costume I'd worn on Saturday over her knees. She kicked a wad of black fabric behind her chair, nudging it out of sight.

"I found a little grass stain near the hemline," she explained quickly, fluffing the blue dress. "Nothing major. I've been working it out."

Must've happened when I'd kneeled in front of that little scarecrow.

"I booked an order for Wednesday. Mrs. Martin needs twenty cookies for her daughter's first grade class in the shape of ghosts. You can make them cute. Give them big smiles and edible glitter. Kids love glitter."

I knocked my hip against the side of the doorjamb, watching as she dabbed at the fabric. "I can start working on the cookies after my homework tonight. I only have one worksheet."

And I already started planning on how I could speed that up. I loved decorating cookies. It was relaxing and creative and fun. Gram always got on my case because I tended to put too much effort into a single cookie, but I couldn't help it.

Gram looked up. Her work glasses made her eyes appear three times larger, bug-eyed by the magnification lenses. I smiled a little, even though she looked at me seriously. "I was putting away your laundry today and found something in your sock drawer."

That smile on my face instantly vanished. "Gram—"

"You never told me your father sent you a letter," she said, holding my gaze as if to freeze me in place. "I also didn't miss that it was unopened."

The letter. Thinking about it left me wincing, a mixture of red-hot anger and cool sadness barreling through me. "I don't want to read it." Even I could tell that my voice almost sounded petulant, like a child.

Those bug eyes widened with sympathy. "Honey, you can't ignore it. He's your father. What if there's something important inside? Like photos, money—"

"I don't need his photos." The vise around my throat made my voice harsher than I'd intended. "I don't need his money. I don't need his letter. Just throw it away."

"You don't have to answer him, Blaire." Gram switched tactics, reaching up to pluck off her glasses. "You can read it, see what he has to say. Maybe he wants to apologize."

Maybe he did. Maybe Dad had written an eloquent apology that'd win some kind of award. After two years of complete radio silence, disappearing in the night with a pathetic scribble of an excuse, the apology had better be epic.

His letter had come in the mail two weeks ago now, and I remembered that day with perfect clarity. One look at the orange envelope's return address, and my whole world had dropped out from underneath me, reminding me how easily people could walk away.

"I don't care why he's writing," I told Gram finally, pushing off the jamb. The choking pressure traveled down my throat, expanding into my chest. I turned on my heel, that icy heat steaming in my veins. *I won't care ever again.*

three

hough I hated Halloween and all it encompassed, I loved decorating the cupcakes and cookies ordered for the month. There was something cathartic about piping out the holiday-themed frosting, creating an image, watching the icing mattify. All of our different parties offered so many different colors and designs—a black witch hat with a bright orange buckle, a pumpkin on a blended background, a mermaid's tail in a glittering sea.

For Mrs. Martin's order, I shaped cookies to look like ghosts, decorated them as Gram had asked—big, goofy smiles, glitter—and even added mustaches to a few, bowties on others, just to make them fun. Cute.

Costume Catering didn't get many walk-in customers, so Gram decided to take a quick trip to the grocery store, leaving me on decorating *and* counter duty. Since it left me in blissful silence, I didn't mind.

On the extra cookies I'd baked, I designed something

different. Instead of one ghost on the cookie, I squeezed together two, their ghostly trails weaving together, eyes angled at each other. I hadn't meant to make the one ghost's eyes blue, the exact shade of Lucas's, but it was too late.

The front door of the shop chimed as someone came through it, the noise startling me so much that my piping bag dug into the surface of my cookie, effectively smearing the blue gaze. Probably for the best.

"One second!" I called, grabbing the hand towel at my elbow and getting to my feet. From where I'd pulled my barstool up, I couldn't see the front door. An opaque partition shielded the front of the shop and the kitchen area so only a shadowy outline peeked through.

When I rounded the screen, I immediately froze.

A part of me actually thought I was imagining Lucas standing in the middle of the front office. Like my insane brain conjured the image of him. Those two blue eyes, identical to the ones on my cookie, looked back at me, causing my heart to kick into an erratic pace.

For a long moment, there was only the hum of the heater and the roar of blood in my ears.

"I know I'm probably the last person you want to see," Lucas said quickly with a strange expression on his face, much different than the teasing glint to his eyes from school this morning. He almost looked *nervous.* "I'm here on business, actually. My mom sent me. I was hoping it'd be Gram in the shop."

"She's not your gram." My response came automatically, devoid of emotion even though my palms started sweating. I slowly wiped at my hands, the sugar and frosting sticking to my fingertips. "And your mom already booked her order a few weeks ago. Cookies and lemonade for this Saturday. She's planning a royal tea party, right?"

"She tried your gram's mini caramel cheesecakes at the last church potluck and loved them."

A small smile tugged at my lips before I could stop it. "Of course she did." Those things were absolute heaven.

"She wanted to add some of those to her order. One-hundred-fifty of them."

My eyes widened. "One-hundred-fifty mini cheesecakes by Saturday? That's short notice."

"I would've asked you before..." Lucas came close enough to lean his jean-clad hip against the edge of the desk, peering at the stack of business cards lined along the surface. Gram didn't keep much up in the front of the office. It was more of a formality space than anything. "But *someone's* pesky cold shoulder prevented any conversation."

He slid his fingers across the countertop, tracing the designs in the marble, trying to look nonchalant, but there was no missing the stiffness in his shoulders, no missing the tension behind his words. I knew him, and he knew me.

I cleared my throat, effectively cutting off the pressure building there. "I can ask Gram, but I don't know if she'll be able to swing it." It was a mean thing for me to say; Gram would've been able to add those cheesecakes to the order with ease. I only didn't trust myself to give him an inch.

"How was the Wilsons party on Saturday?" Lucas asked. "Did you miss your extra set of hands?"

Ah, yes. The *honorary member*, Lucas Avery. He knew about the Wilson party because it had been planned in advance, before we broke up. "We managed perfectly fine."

Only a moment of hesitation passed as Lucas tried to find a new angle to attack from. "My mom's been asking about you, you know. She misses you. Delia too."

I gripped the hand towel tighter, holding it to my chest as if it would suffuse the pain. "Lucas." *Mentioning them is a low blow.*

"Hey, Delia's only nine. You were in her life for almost two years. She's allowed to miss you."

Thinking about his little sister's round face and wide eyes made my guilt even stronger. "It's done. It's over. Let's let things be."

He gave me the look that used to make my knees weak. Thank God I had the desk to hide behind, so the quivering went unnoticed. His voice softened. "Come on, Bee, I miss talking to you. Having you around." He leaned even further forward. "Hearing you yell at me."

"Oh, you want me to yell at you more? Because I can do that."

Though Lucas still had a shadow of a smile, his voice sounded sad, the low timbre a haunting sound. "You're not going to say you miss me, too?"

My grip on the towel tightened until my knuckles went numb.

I loved him. I loved him so much that I almost felt

crazy, like trying to contain such a strong emotion rendered me near insane. The idea of living my life separate from his was a blow to my stomach, knocking the breath out of me.

And that was the problem.

Lucas must've seen something change, because his carefully crafted mask cracked entirely, revealing his raw, pleading expression. "Can we just talk, Blaire? About what happened, about *why*. If I pushed you too far—"

I quickly cut him off, not allowing my brain to process his words. "You didn't." If I went down that road, down memory lane, I wouldn't be able to pull myself back. "It wasn't that."

"If it wasn't that, then *why*?"

Why, why, why. Why had I broken up with the boy I loved to pieces? Why had I thrown both of our lives into a blender and pressed the button?

I couldn't tell him.

So I pulled back, curling my fingers into fists, tucking them in my apron pocket. "Things changed," I told him evenly, pretending to be unaffected. Never before would I have called myself a great actress, but Lucas bought it. Every. Time. I wanted to shake him for it. He didn't respond; only watched me. "I'll have Gram give your mom a call when she gets back in."

I turned away before he could see my face fall, see the pain clear in my gaze.

"Blaire," Lucas called after me, but I didn't stop until I was safely back with my cookies and cupcakes, my ghosts leering at me with their grins. I half expected Lucas to follow me, to come into the kitchen and keep the conversation going, but he didn't.

I gripped the edge of the table with shaking fingers, holding my breath, my lungs straining and burning.

Only when the door chimed and Lucas was gone could I breathe.

When Gram got back to the store, I let her know that Mrs. Avery wanted to add the caramel cheesecakes to her order, only for her to give me a strange look. "I know," she said. "Mrs. Avery asked me at the Sunday potluck, and I told her it wasn't a problem. It isn't, right?"

I drew in a slow breath through my nose, shaking my head ever so slightly. *Nice try, Lucas.* "No problem at all."

One of the perks of living in a small town was there was only one building for the elementary, middle, and high schools. Mrs. Martin didn't mind the idea of me dropping the cookies off to her daughter's class—one less thing she had to do.

I dropped off the Halloween ghosts as soon as I got to school the next day, and I would've given my life for them. It had taken me a while to perfect them—even longer for my hands to stop shaking after Lucas had left.

I easily would've shoved a kid out of the way to protect these cookies.

Well, gently shoved. Nudged, maybe.

Maybe.

But walking out of the elementary hallway and moving

back to the high school wing had me a little weighed down. I dodged kid after wayward kid as they scrambled to unpack their backpacks and get ready for the school day. Halloween-themed decorations lined the tops of the lockers and classroom doors—the mossy kind of spiderwebs and paper witches flying above the doorways. Kids' crafts also hung on the walls in the hall, decorated with hand-print pumpkins and pictures of jack-o-lanterns. A few hung crooked, as if the children themselves had put them up.

See, down in the elementary hallway, Halloween felt fun and exciting. I could see why kids loved it so much.

With all the love for Halloween in the community, I just wished a little could rub off on me.

I'd showed up to school early to drop off the cookies, so I had about ten minutes to kill before I had to make my way to Mr. Miller's room. Not a lot of high schoolers showed this early in the morning, everyone trying to sleep in as much as possible. Donnie would show up soon with our coffees; I had to wait.

I reached behind me for my backpack, grabbing my cell phone to send Gram a quick text. I wanted to let her know that the cookies had been delivered without injury. Knowing Gram, she wouldn't get it until Mrs. Martin called her raving about the treats—Gram hadn't mastered the art of texting yet—but I thought I might as well put the message out there.

But instead of my fingers touching the smooth surface of my cell, I felt something papery and wide. Frowning, I latched on to it, pulling it out. Immediately, everything in me soured.

My dad always wrote his words in capitals, so *Blaire* was emblazoned like a scream across the front of the orange envelope, a festive pumpkin stamp in the top corner. I froze in the middle of the hallway, unable to tear my gaze away from the stupid letter shaking in my grip.

Gram. She must've put it in my backpack. The longer I looked at the letter, the more a bubbling sensation began to rise in my chest.

She thought that as soon as I saw this stupid thing again, it'd be game over. I'd fold. I'd read Dad's letter. I'd write a response. Just by seeing it again, touching it, my resistance would crumble. She was banking on that.

"You okay?"

You have got to be flipping *kidding me.*

Lucas's finger cut into my vision and pointed at the return address. "Is that—"

"Don't." I shrugged his hand away and pressed forward, my steps more like monster stomps in the high school hallway. I gripped the envelope with tight fingers, and it wouldn't surprise me if the stupid thing ripped under the pressure. Good.

"Your dad sent you a letter, huh?" Lucas asked, keeping up with my elephant-like footfalls and following me to my locker. "What does it say?"

"I obviously haven't opened it," I snapped at him, clenching my jaw shut tight. *He only saw the front,* my brain reasoned with my personified anger, trying to coax it back within reasonable boundaries. *He wouldn't have seen that the seal hadn't been broken.* "And I'm not going to."

As I turned down the corridor with my locker, I started toward the trash can.

Gram was wrong. I *wouldn't* open the stupid thing just because she'd packed it in my bag. If she wouldn't throw it away, I would.

I reached to toss the envelope into the trash when Lucas cut around in front of me, body-blocking the garbage can. The familiar teasing glint to his gaze vanished—those blue eyes were serious and trained on me. "Blaire."

"Would you *move*?" I shoved at his chest, but the football player didn't even freaking budge. "Seriously. Move."

"You don't want to throw that away." The edge of his jaw became prominent as his lips tightened. "Open it or don't open it, but don't throw it away. It could have something important inside."

I threw my hands up as everything spilled over. Anger had won out against reason, and it made my tone piercing. "You sound like Gram. This letter? It's none of your business. So, can you drop it? We broke up, and I've been perfectly clear on the fact that I don't want to talk to you. Why don't you go bother someone else?"

Lucas's chest rose sharply and fell once. I waited and waited for a sarcastic remark in return, an eye roll, *something*, but he froze solid. For one heartbeat, two. The paper in my hand became heavier and heavier.

The longer he looked into my eyes, the more exposed I felt. He used to do that all the time—trace my eyes, find the true feelings there. He'd always tell me my words could be fantastic at weaving a lie, but my eyes would give me away. And he looked in them now, trying to decipher the truth, and I couldn't let him.

Don't feel guilty, don't feel guilty.

So I squeezed my eyes shut, heart thumping painfully in my chest.

The night before I'd broken up with Lucas had been the best night of my life.

Lucas's parents and little sister had been out of the house for the night, and I'd gone over to watch movies with him, like we always had when no one was home. There was something about the fact that we were alone that night, in that big house, that made me bold, braver than before.

That night, everything had been charged ten times higher than ever.

I could still remember how it felt to have his lips on my neck as my fingers fumbled for the buttons on his shirt, the warmth of his breath as he'd chuckled against my skin.

Could still remember the near-crushing feeling in my chest of loving him so much.

Could still remember the moment when my cell phone rang, startling us apart.

Could still remember the happy look on his face the next day as he'd sat beside me in the car, moments before I'd broken his heart.

I saw stars from how tightly I pinched my eyes shut, and I dragged in a breath to apologize. When I finally got the courage to look, Lucas no longer stood in front of me.

No, he and his stiff shoulders already headed down the hall.

A strangled sort of compression worked its way up my throat, crawling along the sides, scraping it raw. Desperation made my voice sharp. "Are you going to run away with hurt feelings? What, you can't take it? I thought you *missed* me yelling at you?" *Please stop, please stop,* I thought to him, my breath shaking. If he didn't turn, it might've been the final straw.

That razor-sharp panic ebbed a little as Lucas pulled to a halt, pivoting on his heel. A distance of seven lockers separated us, as well as two students who tried to seem like they weren't eavesdropping.

"You told me to walk away," he said to me, voice level.

But I didn't mean *it.*

The letter in my hand weighed me to the ground, as if made of lead. And the trash bin was right there, right in front of me, but I couldn't even think about dropping it.

I reached around and tucked it back into my backpack, tugging on the zipper as I crossed the distance between us. "I...I shouldn't have said that. Any of that."

"I *do* know we broke up, Blaire," Lucas said quietly, so quietly that the two students listening wouldn't have been able to hear. "I remember I can't walk up to you like I used to. I can't hold you like I used to. I'm not sure why you think it slipped my mind."

"It's this stupid month," I told him, folding my arms, trying to shrug on a coat of nonchalance, one ten sizes too small. I fought so hard to wipe away the sharpness of the moment. "I—I just hate October. I hate Halloween. It puts me in a...bad mood."

"Those are fighting words in these parts. Hallow takes Halloween *very* seriously." He attempted at humor, but the emotion didn't settle in his eyes, his voice too flat. "But I get what you mean."

He *would* know what I meant. He'd been there this time last Halloween, the first anniversary of Dad leaving. He'd been there to witness everything.

"I don't want to pretend you don't exist," I told him honestly, looking up into his eyes even though it was a bad idea. "I'm not used to being around you this way."

Lucas had said he missed being able to walk up to me, being able to hold me the way he used to, and I missed the same things. I missed being able to call him at night and listen to his breathing on the other end of the phone when he fell asleep. I missed playing games with him and Delia in their backyard.

So much history laid between us that the thought of it all going down the drain made me ache. Then again, the thought of holding on to a dead-end hurt even more.

He offered me a smile, making my breath catch. "We could be friends."

I so badly wanted to agree. "That never works, and you know it."

"We could make it work."

"No, we couldn't." Not when my insides tore apart each time I saw him. "It's only been two weeks, Lucas. Not enough time to separate *relationship* and *friendship*."

Lucas took a step forward so only an arm's reach of distance separated us. I kept my arms close to my chest, forbidding them from reaching out. "You said so yourself— you're struggling through this month. You need friends to get you through it."

I took a step back. Distance. Distance was good. "I've got Donnie."

"Got me for what?" Donnie asked as he walked up to the two of us, two cups of coffee in hand. He'd worn his dark hair loose today, no gel to spike it up. He eyed Lucas. "Hey, man. I didn't realize you rejoined the ranks or else I'd have brought you a coffee too."

"He's not rejoining the ranks," I told Donnie as I took my espresso, shaking the mere idea from my head and continuing my trek to my locker. "He's merely being a nuisance."

Donnie's and Lucas's footfalls on the linoleum were harmonious behind me, as well as their following voices. "Don't listen to her—Blaire and I are friends now. Or, should I say, *again.*"

"Friends?" Donnie's voice pitched high.

I couldn't blame him. Donnie had been there through the trenches of our breakup, unsure which side to settle on. He was family, sure, but I was the one who'd broken up with Lucas, his friend, with no explanation. I hadn't told Donnie about why, so he knew nothing.

And with how I'd been lately, if I were him, I'd be nervous about the idea of Lucas and me being friends too.

I took a sip of my espresso and almost immediately spit it out. "Gah, did you put sugar in this?"

"Do you not normally get sugar?" Donnie asked, brow squished.

"You've never put sugar in it before."

He blinked. "Oh. Well, you know, I thought you could use some sweetening," Donnie returned quickly, but he didn't stick to the subject long. "But really. Friends? Why?"

"Because I hate myself, apparently," I muttered, and as I approached my locker, I saw a paper had been taped to the front of it—an orange-colored poster with small decorations on the front. Once I realized what it was, I sighed. "No, the *universe* hates me."

The annual Halloween festival was coming up next Saturday, and of course someone had taped a poster for it on the front of my locker. Out of all the other lockers, they'd chosen mine.

HALLOWEEN BOO-BASH: EAT, DRINK, AND BE SCARY.

Ha. So clever.

I grabbed it, crumpling it up into a ball before dropping it to the ground.

"She hates Halloween," Lucas whispered to Donnie.

I ripped my locker open, my newspaper clippings fluttering in the breeze. Why advertise a community event at school, anyway? They didn't have to advertise on *my locker*, either.

"How can someone not like Halloween?" Donnie demanded, and I looked over my shoulder. He sipped at his coffee, looking cheery. "It's the best holiday. Well, second to Christmas."

I narrowed my eyes at him. "Your pumpkin spice is giving me a headache."

"Plus, the Boo-Bash is the best, Blaire. Everyone around here treats it like a second prom. It's, like, the biggest event of the fall, and you know it."

I did know it, and I dreaded it every year. "Sounds like torture."

"Just saying, if you fully experienced Halloween instead of locking yourself in your bedroom, you'd like it." Donnie gestured at me. "I mean, look at you. You have a skull-and-crossbones backpack. You have creepy pictures in your locker. How do you hate the spookiest month of the year?"

As I hung my bag on the hook, I realized he wasn't wrong. The paper clippings on my locker wall were of strange things—owls with glowing eyes, dark forests, broken stepping stones in a walkway. Random things I'd found as I flipped through magazines and cut out. I guess they could've been a little bit spooky.

I hadn't always hated Halloween. Once upon a time, I'd enjoyed it. That felt like a lifetime ago.

I shook my head. "Just because I like the aesthetic of it doesn't mean I have to like the month."

"Donnie's right," Lucas said, tapping his fingers against my open locker door. His gaze traced over the clippings and taped pictures. "If you fully experienced Halloween, you'd love it."

"What the heck does 'fully experiencing Halloween' mean?" It sounded creepy. And exhausting.

"You just need help to see the greatness in the holiday," he said, eyebrows rising and falling. "Help from your *friends*."

My first instinct was to scoff, loudly and in his face, but I found myself stilling under his azure gaze as it focused down at me. Sarcasm coated my voice thickly. "You're saying you want to show me the joy of pumpkins and ghosts?"

"I'm saying I'm willing to help cure you of your bitterness."

"God knows she's got a lot of it," Donnie quipped.

Lucas's attention lifted over my head to flash my cousin a grin. My coffee warmed my hands, searing my fingers. Donnie had forgotten to get a sleeve.

I didn't want to be the grouch of Halloween, didn't want to put a damper on the holiday, but this was a slippery slope.

I could be strong enough, though. Spending time with Lucas didn't mean things went back to how they were. I could be strong enough to remember why I'd done what I had in the first place—I had enough self-discipline.

My gaze leveled with Lucas's. "You have three chances to convince me October doesn't suck. Three outings."

"Five."

"What? No. You don't get to negotiate terms."

Lucas, though, wasn't stopping. "Four."

Donnie made a noise. "Definitely four. Gram taught you how to compromise, Blaire."

I could've smacked him. He was supposed to be on *my side*. "Fine. Four chances, and Donnie has to be present for every one of them."

"You don't trust me?" Lucas asked, batting his dark and beautiful lashes.

More like I don't trust myself.

"Hey, I don't mind tagging along on your soul-searching journey," Donnie said, shrugging. "As long as there are no haunted houses."

"Deal." Lucas plucked my espresso from my numb fingertips. He had it half raised to his mouth before he paused. "You weren't going to drink this, right?"

I wasn't. Donnie had killed the coffee with sweetness. The only thing worse than a sweet coffee was a letter from my long-lost father, and I had one of those too. Sitting in my backpack. Taunting me. Haunting me.

But there was something about watching Lucas place his lips on the spot where my own had been, the thought of the hot liquid pooling in his mouth. A flash of heat warmed my veins, followed by an icy chill.

I didn't even say anything when I slammed my locker shut, practically running away from the two of them. This time, though, when I walked away, neither boy followed.

four

I struggled on my homework that night, my thoughts trailing from calculus questions to everything else going on. I felt bitter. Pessimistic. Negative. It was like I couldn't help it. Everything that came from my mouth was just...cynical. Recalling how I'd spoken to Lucas today physically hurt, a knife stabbing my insides. I would've thought he'd be the last person I'd speak that way to, but no.

Even down to Mrs. Wilson's costume party last Saturday. I'd been annoyed too. And because of, what—my pinching shoes? What was up with that?

I rubbed my fingers into my eyes with a groan. I blamed it on Dad's stupid letter. Things had been going so well before I'd gotten it. I'd been coming off of the best summer since Mom had died, Lucas and I had been dating happily for over a year, and my junior year of high school had loomed on the horizon. Everything had been perfect, up until I'd pulled that ugly envelope out of the mailbox. And then my world fell apart.

A sharp shriek echoed through the apartment, though slightly muffled through my closed bedroom door, causing me to jerk my pen across my worksheet. "Gram?" I shouted, heart drumming into high-gear, and I shoved to my feet. "Gram! Are you okay?"

I threw my door open when she didn't answer me, bursting into the living room. With the scream still echoing in my ears, I expected to see Gram's small body crumpled on the floor from a heart attack or her finger sliced open from a kitchen knife. *Something.*

Instead, she sat at the kitchen table, laptop open in front of her, a wide grin on her face.

"Jeez," I muttered, pressing a palm to my chest. My heart didn't want to settle down, not yet. "I thought you broke a hip or something, Gram."

That wide grin faltered, but only slightly. "Oh, I'm not that old. Come look, quick!"

"Did you open up a spam email again?" I asked, rounding the table. "I told you not to click on anything if you don't recognize who sent it."

Gram pointed a frail finger on the computer, not caring how her fingerprints would transfer onto the screen. "Just look, would you?"

I looked, and immediately figured out why she'd screamed.

The subject line read ***Halloween Boo-Bash Catering Request***.

Of flipping course.

"They're asking *me* to cater!" she exclaimed, fidgeting in her seat. "Or, well, *us*, but still! This is huge, Blaire. They usually always hire out some fancy bigwig company from Bayview."

"'Bout time they went local," I huffed, and though her excitement was so exuberant, I couldn't quite get myself to share it. I pushed off the table, heading to the fridge. "Can you make it fit into your schedule? It's so last minute."

"Of course I can make it fit! This is the Boo-Bash we're talking about." She leaned forward, reading the email with her mouth wide open.

The amazingly wonderful Boo-Bash. Ugh. It was bad enough the party had been advertised on my locker—now we had to cater it, too? I guess I couldn't avoid it this year.

I went to the fridge to pour myself a glass of soda, the kitchen holding a stifling sort of silence, nothing but the fizz of my pop filling the air. "I'm happy for you, Gram," I forced out after a moment, looking at where she sat. "This *is* huge for you."

"It's going to be amazing. I can wear my fairy godmother costume—you know, the one that makes me look taller?—and you can wear the princess gown—"

A groan slipped out. "Can't Donnie wear it this time?"

There was something childlike about wearing costumes around other adults. Sure, they wore costumes too, but it still felt strange. Like I was playing dress-up. Like *their* costumes were appropriate because they were at a party, but my pretty, pretty princess gown was weird because I wasn't a guest. I was a *worker*. It probably wouldn't have been so bad if I could've dressed up as something else— something more festive for the time of year—but *no*.

Gram rolled her eyes. "I'm not sure he'd look as lovely as you do in it."

"Why can't I be a ghost?" I demanded. "More of a Halloween staple?"

"I can probably whip together a pumpkin costume if you wanted. Something large and unflattering."

Honestly, it would've been better than the princess dress.

Gram peered over her shoulder at me, the glow of the computer screen a faded shadow around her figure. "Blaire," she said, tone changing in an instant, going from excited to almost nervous, "I'll understand if you don't want to work the Bash. I know...I know how hard this time of year is for you. Especially since..."

A fist of discomfort clenched my stomach, but I flipped my switch. The smile I pulled onto my face *felt* real enough —real enough to fake her out. "It's a big party for you, Gram. You're going to need all hands on deck. Besides, I haven't been in years. It'll be fun to go again, rather than watching it from my window."

For a moment, I felt bad about lying to her, for pulling on a phony smile to brush off her concern. That moment of guilt quickly washed away as a relieved look crossed her expression, and I knew I'd made the right choice.

· · ·

I was freezing my butt off. And for what?

A stupid football game.

"This counts as one of our outings," I grumbled to Donnie, but he probably couldn't even hear me over the noise of the bleacher section cheering on the team. The Hallow High Devils—for a town that loved Halloween, that mascot was no surprise—led the game by over ten points in the last quarter, and yet whenever we got the ball, our side of the football field acted like we made the winning touchdown. By the end of the night, my eardrums would be goo.

"It doesn't count," Donnie replied to me. "Lucas isn't here."

"Uh, yes he is. He's—" I pointed to the football field with all the players, "—down there. He's present and accounted for, meaning this totally counts."

Okay, so he wasn't *exactly* accounted for. At least, not the entire time. I had trouble finding his jersey number over the jolly giant standing in front of me, eclipsing my view.

Donnie glanced sideways at me. His black hair curled out from underneath his knit cap, his dark trench coat pulled up around his neck. "You used to love football games. You used to wear orange-and-black face paint like the players and cheer your boyfriend on. What happened to that girl?"

That girl had run out of paint and broken up with Lucas.

When Donnie had asked me to come to tonight's football game, a part of me *had* wanted to come. Not that I'd ever admit that aloud. It was the last football game of the season—the last football game of Lucas's high school career. I didn't want to be able to say that I'd missed one of the biggest nights in Lucas's senior year.

And I *really* hated myself for caring, because I was about to turn into a human popsicle.

"It feels weird being here," I told him, glancing around.

"I bet. You haven't been to a game all season, have you?"

No, I hadn't. Not even homecoming. "I only ever came to these things for Lucas."

Again, I could feel Donnie looking sideways at me. This time, I kept my focus on the field, watching our orange-and-black team bob and weave through the blue-and-gray players. The football bounced somewhere in the mix, lost to me. "He told me he looks for you in the crowd every game."

"You don't have to tell me those things," I said a little sharply, digging my fingers into my palms. The effect was somewhat lost through the barrier of my thin mittens. "It's not...helpful." The opposite, actually.

"Come on, Blaire." He sighed, his breath fogging in the air. "This is ridiculous, you know. Why won't you tell me what happened between you two? Maybe I can help."

"I told you. Irreconcilable differences."

"Please. You and Mr. Dreamy practically never fought. About anything serious, anyway. You two were head over heels for each other."

"And doesn't that sound unhealthy to you?" I demanded, my voice quivering as it rose. None of the people around us seemed to be listening, but I fought to control my volume. "Never fighting with someone?"

Donnie faced me fully, eyebrows pulled low on his eyes. "You know what's unhealthy? This." He gestured at me with both hands. "You. All of you. I've never seen you like this, Blaire. Never. And I've known you for a long time."

I focused my stony gaze on everywhere but him. "You know October's hard for me." My words hardened. "Have you ever thought maybe I'm in a bad mood because of what time of the year it is?"

"I get it, I do, but your bad mood caused you to dump your boyfriend, who you were totally in love with up until the night you broke it off, so I'm just a little confused."

I'd never wished more that I could be invisible. That Donnie couldn't see me and I could be silent, to not have such questions hanging in the air, to not be called out in a way like this. Because even though I refused to look at him, I could still feel *him* looking at *me*, trying to probe out the truth.

As the clock ticked down, a player with an orange jersey stepped over the line at the end of the field, causing the entire section of the bleachers to erupt in a colossal noise of applause and cheers. I flinched at the suddenness of it, pulling back as someone elbowed my side.

"I'm going to the bathroom," I told Donnie, making sure he wouldn't follow.

It was colder tonight, cold enough for goosebumps to raise underneath my thin jacket. It usually took Hallow a little while to cool down from our summers, but this year, the chill settled faster. It'd be a cold Halloween. Kids' costumes would be half obscured by their jackets and gloves, feebly trying to warm them. All the effort on their parents' part to keep them best dressed would be in vain, since the cool fall breeze would win.

I sucked down deep breaths of air, crunching the dropped popcorn with the soles of my shoes. Lost in my thoughts, I took the corner of the bleachers too sharply and ran straight into someone. Someone small. Reeling back, I blinked hard. "Delia?"

Lucas's little sister looked a lot like him, in a way. Her cheeks were a little rounder, but her eyes were the same. Both of theirs held the same curve, but Delia's were hidden behind small pink glasses. The stadium lights reflected in them.

"Hi, Blaire," she said with a small smile, one that hesitantly graced her lips. She held a packet of popcorn, a thick layer of orange cheese-salt sitting on the top. "They're giving away free popcorn since the game's almost over."

I nodded, a bittersweet feeling working through me. I missed her almost as much as I missed Lucas. Almost. "Very cool. Looks like you've got a lot of salt there."

"The lid broke on the shaker."

Despite everything, my lips twitched. "Here." I took the packet of popcorn from her and grabbed the edges at the top, giving it a good shake. "If you do this, some of the salt falls to the bottom."

When I handed the popcorn back, her hesitant smile

turned into something much more genuine, much more familiar. "Thanks." She shook the bag a little bit, trying the new trick out. "I haven't seen you in so long. You never come over anymore."

"I've just been so busy lately." *Great, now I'm lying to children.*

Delia shifted the bag of popcorn, not looking at me. "You know, Lucas is sad a lot at home. I think he misses you coming around, too."

A lick of pain flared up in my chest, and though I tried to shy away from it, it was unavoidable. I reached over and swiped a piece of her popcorn, wincing as a burst of salt coated my tongue. "I'm coming over tomorrow for your mom's party. I'll see both of you then."

"Really?" It was almost comical how fast her head whipped up, her glasses falling low on her nose. "Mom didn't tell me that. I'll have to clean my room. She says I can't have friends in there when it's so messy, which is super lame. I'll definitely get it cleaned by tomorrow, because we painted my room a few weeks ago, and I want to show you." Delia paused, as if aware she'd been speaking quickly. "If you want to see it."

"Of course I want to see it," I told her, nudging her shoulder. "But don't tell me the color—I want to be surprised."

Delia nodded, her hair bobbing in its ponytail. "Deal. I'll see you tomorrow."

As she hurried off with a bounce to her step, the game buzzer sounded, loud and echoing in the night, signaling the game was over. From where I stood, I couldn't see the scoreboard, but I knew from how loud the Hallow section cheered that we'd won.

The last game of the season. The last game of Lucas's high school career.

The line for the bathroom was long, and I took my time washing my hands, enjoying the idea of Donnie waiting around trying to find me in the mass of people filtering towards their cars. He might've been right; my bitter emotions were probably a little unhealthy. At this moment, though, punishing him for saying it felt good.

Which was so wrong.

However, when I emerged from the bathroom, pulling back on my mittens, karma hit me in the face like a slap.

Lucas leaned on one of the stone benches by the edge of the football field's fence. He held his shoulder pads by the collar, his black shirt hugging his torso tightly, leaving nothing to the imagination. The sweat in his hair made it curl slightly at the ends, appearing a lot darker than its normal chocolate color. He still wore his football pants, which hugged his thighs and hips snugly.

All the air vanished from my lungs.

But as my laser-focus on Lucas faded, I realized someone stood in front of him. Someone petite. Brunette. She had her back to me, so I couldn't see who it was, but I did see when she touched his arm. The slow-motion movement tortured my brain. Five fingers on his skin for longer than five seconds. I couldn't help but count.

Another girl stood in the mix of conversation. She had

her cell phone out, poised as if taking a picture. No, she *was* taking a picture. Of the brunette and Lucas.

It was like I was watching this scene unfold outside of my body. I had zero reaction as the brunette turned to my direction, her face coming into full view. *Hailey Moore.*

She was a grade above me, in Lucas's class, and on the cheer squad. Her uniform matched Lucas perfectly. A hot football player and pretty cheerleader couple.

Another fun fact about Hailey? She and Lucas had dated his sophomore year. Which was fantastic.

Hailey flipped her hair over her shoulder before leaning into Lucas's side, so close that not an inch separated them. She even put one of her hands on Lucas's flat chest, taking any and every excuse to touch him.

At last, Lucas's eyes shifted to the left and found mine.

You gave him up, I reminded myself, but my thoughts were quiet, as if I whispered in the dark. A shiver tore down my spine, and I wasn't sure it was from the cold. *You let him go.*

I schooled my features into a mask of blankness, sure that not a trace of expression remained as I held Lucas's gaze. I couldn't stand there, couldn't watch some other girl touch him like I used to. If I did, I'd let myself remember how he smelled after a game, how his chest felt as I pressed my fingers there, how his smile widened to show his teeth just for me.

So I turned on my heel and walked away, balling my hands into fists so tight that my nails tried to cut through the material of my mittens.

"Blaire." Lucas was there, at my side, his earthy scent following him. His hair matted along the skin at his temples, pressed down by the damp. Those blue eyes were crystalline, wide, and focused on me. "Bee, that wasn't—"

I immediately threw a hand up, trying not to let him see my discomfort. Hearing him try to explain himself when he'd done nothing wrong made me feel *icky*, as well as being caught staring. Both cringe-inducing. "I thought it was sweet. Who knew you were so popular?"

"She wanted a picture," he said, shaking his head a little, as if the mere idea was ludicrous. "She said she wanted to remember her senior year."

"Yeah, right. Or she wanted the picture to post on her social media and make everyone think you're a couple again."

Lucas shifted his hold on his shoulder pads, looking straight into my eyes. "I don't care what everyone thinks."

I needed to get out of there before I said something stupid, because my body felt all kinds of traitorous. My heartbeat thumped unevenly inside my chest, my lungs deciding they didn't want oxygen. *Traitorous.* You'd think the sight of a guy sweaty would be gross, but *dang*.

I took a deliberate step back from him. "I need to go find Donnie. He's probably waiting for me." *Or he left without me, in which case, punishing him totally backfired.*

"I'm surprised you came tonight," Lucas threw out quickly, following my retreat. As if he knew if he kept talking, I'd stay and listen. "You haven't been to a game all season."

With another step back, my back came dangerously close to pressing against the side of the bathroom outer wall. "I wasn't going to miss your last game."

Lucas advanced further. "Why not?"

"Because it's important to you." I curled my hands into fists. "And that's what a *friend* would do, right?"

Ah, the f-word. A hail-Mary, a yellow flag on the play to make this game stop, if only for a moment. I couldn't breathe, not with him so close, with the scent of memories clinging to his skin.

It didn't do much to faze him, though. In fact, my words almost encouraged him to smile wider. "So it's official, huh? I'm your friend."

"Don't know what I was thinking."

"You miss me." The words came out almost as a whisper as he drew nearer, the blue in his eyes heating until the color looked like silk. "I'd have to say the feeling's mutual, Bee."

My chest tightened as I gazed up at him, at the red lines around his neck from where his shoulder pads had rubbed at his skin. I wanted to reach out and trace my fingertips along the lines, to feel the heat of his skin in contrast to the cool October air. My memory proved a sweet sort of torture, giving me a shadow of a reminder of how his touch once felt, but not with enough clarity that left me satisfied. No, just enough to make me crazy.

"You should go catch up with Hailey," I told him, words coming out petty. "Take her out for some coffee or something. Help her remember her senior year a little more clearly."

Your insecurity is showing, my thoughts hissed.

Lucas remained quiet for a moment as he watched me, examining my expression, but I was almost positive my mask still rested in place. "Why don't you and I get coffee?" he asked after a moment, taking a play from my book and ignoring what I'd said. "Celebrate the last win of the season."

"Donnie's looking for me." My response came automatically, and I scoured the crowd behind him. "He's—"

"Blaire." And then five fingertips touched the smooth skin of my cheek, angling my face back to him. A faint sensation, barely there, but even that had my heart skipping a beat. "Come with me?"

I didn't know what did it. Maybe the fact that this was the closest we'd been since our breakup? The way his voice had angled upon the question, tinged with hope? Seeing him posing for a picture with his ex?

Whatever it was, it summoned a pressure to build in my throat, choking off the air, stinging at my eyes. All of my snark went out the window, fleeing into the night. "I can't, Lucas."

I expected him to look sad, disappointed, but he almost had a wistful sort of quality to his expression. Lucas pulled his hand away, taking a full step back. "I'll see you tomorrow, then. At Mom's tea party."

I wanted to ask him what an eighteen-year-old boy was going to be doing at a costume tea party, but this time, I kept my mouth shut. *Don't prolong this more than you need to,* my brain told me, trying to be helpful and logical. My heart didn't want to listen. "Goodnight, Lucas."

"Night, Bee," he returned, and took a few more steps backward before he walked away.

As soon as he did turn around, though, a weight pressed down on my shoulders, sinking me into the ground. I couldn't get the image of Hailey's body against his out of my head. I couldn't help but wonder that if I kept pushing him away, would I be pushing him into the arms of someone else? And if I did, would I be able to endure it?

The answer was obvious, clear, but not simple. Of course I'd endure it. I had no other choice.

five

*I*f I were to write a letter to my dad, it'd go something like this:

Dear ~~Dad~~ Robert (no, not Dad, definitely not Dad),

Let's be real for a second. You left me. Two months after Mom died, you dumped me with Gram and vanished from the face of the earth. I lost one parent, and then the other left me. You suck. There's nothing more to say than that.

I wish you none of the best,
Blaire

A part of me wanted to write that letter anyway, send it to him without even reading the one he'd given me.

The day Dad had left, things seemed normal. He was due to go back to work after he'd used up all his vacation time, and I remember he hadn't been thrilled about it. Only a few days before he was supposed to go back, I'd caught him pulling clothes out of his dresser drawer. "Just reorganizing," he'd said, not looking my way. "Go pack some of your things. We're going to Gram's tonight."

It wasn't unusual for us to stay at Gram's. Dad hated sleeping at the house after Mom was gone, hardly ever stepping foot into his bedroom. We'd both packed our things and had gone to Gram's apartment, and of course she'd welcomed us with open arms. Dad had slept on the couch while I'd slept in the guest room, the one that would soon become my permanent bedroom.

When I'd woken up the morning of Halloween, Dad was gone with only a note left behind to explain his absence. *Blaire, you know I love you. I can't be in Hallow anymore. I'm sorry.*

Three sentences. Fourteen words. And that was it.

When Mom died, never in a thousand years had I thought I'd lose Dad too. Without her, it would've been him and me against the world. It *should've* been him and me against the world. We would've found our new normal eventually, if he'd given it time.

Something I'd never asked Gram, something I'd never said aloud, was *why*. Why hadn't Dad taken me with him? I could understand the desire to escape Hallow, but he'd lost his wife—why would he *willingly* leave me behind? His only daughter. His only child. *Me*.

How could he just...leave me?

Gram had tried to get me to go to therapy, but I was

fine. I'd come to terms with my mother's death—my father's abandonment—my new normal. Fine.

At least, until I'd gotten Dad's letter on October 1st, and then everything had self-destructed.

My relationship with Lucas no longer had been this beautiful thing I could bask in the warmth of—no, it had turned into a ticking time bomb. If I didn't dismantle it, who knew when it'd blow up? Who knew how severe the damage would be?

It sounded crazy, breaking up with someone you were still in love with, but Lucas was graduating this year. What would happen when he went off to college? Met other college girls, saw life outside of Hallow? And besides, if I'd learned one thing in these past two years, it was that nothing was permanent. Nothing lasted. Not even I love you's.

I could thank my parents for that lesson.

Usually adult parties were more refined than kid parties, which made sense. When older people booked the snacks for their parties, they usually placed the order for mimosas and the fancy cucumber crackers. They'd ask for cake pops instead of cupcakes, cheesecake instead of chocolate cake. Usually, we were requested to wear our black catering uniforms—no costumes or colors of any kind.

For most of the adult parties Gram catered, the atmosphere was sophisticated.

Mrs. Avery's party was none of the above.

It was a "royal tea party," but I didn't know if Mrs. Avery tried playing off of a "royals gone wild" theme or what, because there was nothing elegant about this. Someone set up several tea tables throughout her large yard, covered with wild-patterned tablecloths and place-mats, all mismatching. She even had a balloon arch with different-colored balloons. Streamers hung from the low branches of the two trees, swaying delicately in the wind. When the guests arrived, Mrs. Avery had plastic tiaras and crowns passed around.

It reminded me a little bit of a cartoon, with all the bright streamers and tablecloths. A parody of a tea party, in a way.

And I loved every second of it. Even though I had to wear my horrible heels.

I stood in the Avery kitchen, mixing yet another pitcher of the blue-raspberry flavored lemonade, listening to the sound of the metal whisk hitting the glass. No one lingered in the house—everyone entertained themselves in the yard—so I'd successfully found a moment of peace and quiet.

Which was saying something, since I'd been on edge ever since Gram and I had gotten here. Lucas might've been wandering around here somewhere, and the idea of running into him turned my spine into goo.

"How's it coming?" Gram asked as she came in from the back door, holding an empty pitcher. Her costume was something from the renaissance era, or themed like it, the dress red with pale parchment-colored stripes running down the length of her sides. "I'm going to need another one. They're downing it out there. Mrs. Hart practically drank this whole pitcher. I also didn't miss how much champagne she poured into her glass, either."

"Of course she did," I said with a confident smile, pulling out the whisk.

Gram reached for the pitcher in front of me. "I'll take this one. Can you mix up another and bring it out?"

"Yes, ma'am. More lemonade coming up."

"Don't forget the ratios," she reminded me, grabbing the lemonade and heading for the door. "Four-to-one."

I waved her out of the kitchen as I moved to the fridge, my heels clicking on the tile floor. Mrs. Avery was kind enough to let us keep our supplies stocked in her kitchen, making it so much easier than carting around coolers or even driving the food truck.

Uncle John and Aunt Aimee usually manned the food truck whenever we ran it—Gram got too nervous driving it and felt too isolated working in it. Since Donnie and his family had plans today, Mrs. Avery let us steal some of her refrigerator space.

I pulled out the lemon juice, filtered water, and the frozen raspberries from the fridge, carrying all the items to the counter. Gram always raved about her four-to-one ratio of water to lemon juice, but ever since she'd handed over lemonade-making duty to me, I secretly used a ratio of three-to-one. She'd say that was too sour, but since this was the fourth pitcher of lemonade I'd stirred up today, I had a feeling I'd gotten it right.

"Hey, Blaire."

I jumped at the sound of Delia's voice, finding her in the doorway of the kitchen. She hung back, one arm crossed over her pink dress to rub her other one. Someone—probably her mother—had braided her hair to look like a crown on her head.

"You're quiet," I said, looking closely at her expression. Just like last night, she seemed reserved, almost nervous. "I didn't even hear you walk up."

"I couldn't decide what I wanted to wear." Her attention locked onto the pitcher in front of me and all the ingredients I'd laid out on the counter. "Are you making your lemonade?"

"Yep. Do you want to help me?"

That shook some of the nervousness out of her. "Sure. I always love your lemonade." Delia went over to the breakfast bar side of the island and grabbed a barstool, dragging it noisily across the floor. "You used to make it a lot last summer."

"Your brother didn't like it, though. He said it was too sour." I could still remember how his lips had puckered the first time he'd tried it.

Delia rolled her eyes. "That's because he's too sweet."

"Can someone be too sweet?"

She knelt on the top of the barstool, leaning her forearms onto the countertop. "Oh, yeah. Like when they're so sweet that it makes you want to puke. Like double-chocolate cookies. Yuck."

A startled laugh ripped its way out of me as I uncapped

the container of sugar. "I think you're the only kid I know who doesn't like double-chocolate cookies, Delia."

Delia kicked her feet against the edge of the barstool, tossing her head to the side. "Lucas doesn't like them, either."

"Can you pass me the lemon juice?" I could've easily reached the bowl, but I wanted her to feel useful. She wrapped her hands around it and slowly edged it over, hardly sloshing the juice at all. I rinsed the pitcher out before bringing it back to the countertop. After setting the measuring cup in front of Delia, I told her to portion out one full scoop. "So what's new with you? How's school?"

"It's all right," she said with a shrug. "This month has been fun with all the Halloween crafts and stories and everything. We have a costume party next Friday, where we're going to go trick-or-treating to every classroom."

"That does sound fun."

"Yeah. Spencer and I are going to dress up as old people." She tried to hide a smile, pressing her palm against her face. "Mom's taking me to the store soon to get a costume."

"Spencer?" I couldn't help but chuckle a little bit at her crush, her little third-grade romance. Adorable. In the third grade, I'd had two crushes: Tommy Creston and Lucas Avery. "Is he nice?"

Delia's little cheeks turned red, and the color traveled down her neck. "I guess."

"Is he your best friend?"

She made sure not to meet my eye, her face only deepening in color. "I guess."

The thought still had me smiling, but I decided to let the topic pass. After mixing in the lemon juice and the water, I reached for our special blue raspberry syrup. "You know, if you wanted, you could come over to the apartment and look at our costume room. I don't think Gram would mind. You might find something fun for your look."

"That would be totally cool!" She gasped, giving me a disbelieving smile. "Oh my gosh, I've always wanted to go in there. I bet your Gram has so much cool old-people stuff."

"Delia Ann," a voice said, tone properly chastising. "That wasn't nice at all."

Once again, I jumped at the new voice, nearly upsetting the pitcher of lemonade.

Delia let out a sigh. "Mom, I said *cool* old-people stuff. Cool is a good thing."

"I'm more concerned with the phrase *old people*," Mrs. Avery said, shutting the sliding glass door to the backyard behind her.

She wore a dress that came down to mid-calf, a silky sort of material that looked both elegant and comfortable. It was a vibrant, ugly orange color, and that made it even better. She must've taken markers or something to it, because stripes of purple and green were drawn all over the fabric, not opaque enough to be paint.

Mrs. Avery's expression softened as she looked at me. "Blaire, it's so good to see you. I've been meaning to come over and speak with you, but these people will not let me sneak away. I told them I had to go to the bathroom—no one wanted to follow me then."

My laugh probably came out much more nervous than I wanted it to.

In all honesty, the idea of speaking with her made me jittery. Even though she was nice, she *was* Lucas's mom. Donnie had taken my side in the breakup because he was family; surely Mrs. Avery had an opinion about how everything had gone down.

I glanced to my side. "Delia's been helping me make my famous lemonade."

I dumped in the appropriate amount of sugar, and Delia grabbed the spoon to stir everything together. Mrs. Avery and I watched her movements, all three of us quiet enough for the voices outside to filter inside.

"Can I run it out to Gram, Blaire? I promise I'll be careful."

My gaze automatically shifted to Mrs. Avery's. If Delia took it outside, I'd be left alone with her mom—and who knew how that'd go? But if I said no, Delia would shut down, even more than she'd already been around me. And since I didn't have a good excuse, I found myself nodding.

"Be *extra* careful, Delia," her mother told her. "It's glass."

"Oh, it'll be fine." Delia hopped off the barstool and held her hands out. The pitcher wasn't filled too close to the top, but she still walked slowly to the back door, which her mother pulled open for her.

I moved to put the ingredients back into the fridge, tense. My dress fluttered along my legs, the itchy tulle scratching my skin. I frantically flipped through my brain for something to say—*what a nice day for October? Your dress is very creative?*—something to alleviate the pressure that hung in the air. Part of me even wished she'd head back outside and leave me to my silence.

What should I say to my ex-boyfriend's mother? Confrontation was *so* not my thing.

When I turned around to find her still staring, my mouth moved before I had a chance to stop it. "It feels weird being back here. Almost like things haven't changed."

Yeah, great. I really shouldn't have said *that*.

"We've missed you around here," she replied, not commenting on the fact that it was my fault for the changed circumstances. "Lucas told me you guys were trying to be friends again."

"He did?"

"Well, I may have asked." She came up to lean against the edge of the counter, resting her forearms on its surface. "I asked him if he knew your grandmother was catering the party, and he said you two had talked. I pried the rest out of him."

I could practically imagine that scenario going down in my head. "He's trying to convince me to love October."

"With only one week left in the month?"

"Well, more so Halloween, actually. I don't enjoy either one."

"Don't say that around here," Mrs. Avery teased.

"Especially not out there. Those people live and breathe Halloween. They might use your body as a lawn decoration."

She sounded like Lucas. I found myself without a response, not wanting to say the wrong thing. I'd been doing that a lot lately.

"How have you been?" she asked after a moment of quiet. "I think about you and your grandmother this time of the year."

Instinctively, I flinched. A small twitch, probably not one Mrs. Avery even picked up on, but I couldn't repress it. "We're okay," I said slowly. That wasn't a conversation I wanted to talk about with her—with anyone ever. "I should get back outside, see if Gram needs any help."

Mrs. Avery stepped in between me and the door, her eyes soft. They weren't like Delia's or Lucas's—blue as the morning sky—but brown, the color of tree bark after it rained, and they looked into mine. "I think it's a good thing you two are trying to be friends again," she said. Mrs. Avery reached out and grabbed my hand. Her fingers grounded me to the moment. "He needs someone. Someone other than those meat-headed football player friends of his."

I raised a teasing eyebrow. "'Meat-headed football player' is a lot ruder than calling someone 'old.'"

Mrs. Avery's tentative smile broke into her normal grin, the wave of nervousness in me finally starting to recede.

"Hey."

I'd know that voice anywhere.

Lucas had materialized against the kitchen's archway as

if he knew we'd been talking about him. His gaze passed between me and his mom, no doubt judging our outfits. His, though, wasn't so bad. The pair of joggers he wore hung low on his hips, his black shirt accentuating his bronzed skin.

Seeing him pose with Hailey last night felt like a lifetime ago. All those emotions that festered underneath my skin, boiling to a searing degree, were absent now. I didn't feel any jealousy, not when he looked like that and only I got to witness it.

Mrs. Avery's hand squeezed mine once before falling away. "What are you doing out of your room? I told you that you couldn't come out unless you put on your costume."

He looked unamused. "I'm not wearing some lame prince outfit, Mom."

"It's a *costume party*."

"I can see that." His eyes slid my way.

Yeah, I felt ten kinds of ridiculous in this princess dress, and him noticing as well did nothing to dull that embarrassment. Not like he could've missed the fluffy blue dress anyway, with the chiffon scratching at my skin, and the two braided blonde buns at the top of my head.

"I should get back to my guests," Mrs. Avery said after a moment, heading to the back door. At the last moment, she turned, her orange dress fluttering. "I'd love to talk with you more sometime, Blaire. I miss hearing your voice in this house." With that, she went back outside.

"She's a little much," Lucas said after Mrs. Avery shut

the door behind her. He still lingered in the doorway with his arms crossed, the most familiar stance I'd seen him hold lately. I didn't have to be a psychology whiz to know what that meant. His body was on defense, ready to protect itself at anything that came its way. Probably ready for any searing words I'd potentially throw. "She's been so excited about today. She even had that costume laid out on my bed when I got out of the shower."

"You should've put it on," I told him. "It would've been festive."

One eyebrow rose. "Those pants looked way too tight in certain places, if you get my drift."

"No excuses." I glanced out the window that hung above the kitchen sink, peering out into the backyard. Parties like this were hard for me to keep engaged with. We weren't constantly serving hors d'oeuvres or anything like that. Mrs. Avery had a table with desserts on it, and we made more lemonade. In reality, we didn't need to be present. We could've dropped off the cheesecakes and cookies and gone home.

But this meant something to Gram. It was her way of getting out, getting around people. This filled her cup of extroverted-ness. It drained mine.

"You look really pretty," Lucas said, pulling me from my thoughts. He unhinged himself from the doorway and finally came deeper into the kitchen. He was barefoot, foot-steps soundless. "I know it's for the party, and I know it's only a costume, but you look beautiful."

Heat swamped and fluttered through my chest, those

words awakening the sensation I used to always feel with him. I told myself it was all superficial. Residual butterflies that had been hibernating. They'd die, with time. "It's so itchy," I said with an unaffected voice, pretending like his compliment didn't affect me. "And the shoes suck."

Lucas leaned forward to watch as I lifted the hem of my dress, exposing the plastic shoes. They were tinted a blue color, so he couldn't see my squished toes, but I could sure feel it. "They don't suck on you."

Die, butterflies, die.

"I would've thought you'd be breathing down my neck with Halloween activities," I told him, taking the steering wheel of the subject and turning it sharply. The countertop between us provided a good buffer for my brain, gave me a little bit of clarity inside my bubble of personal space. "You know, hayrides, pumpkin carvings. You've only got a week left to change my mind that this isn't the worst holiday ever."

He took a seat at one of the barstools on the other side of the counter, propping his elbow. "Good thing I've got something booked tonight."

"Tonight?" That was news to me. "We can't. Donnie's doing something with his family."

"Donnie's free after seven," Lucas said, "and then we're hanging out."

I glanced at the clock readout on the microwave, frowning. "I've got to help Gram get all the dishes back home, help her clean up—"

Lucas cut me off. "I've already cleared it with Gram.

She called this morning to double-check on stuff with Mom, and I spoke with her. Asked if you could get off early tonight. She said yes."

Of course she'd said yes. And of course Lucas had talked to her. As soon as I got home tonight, she'd bombard me with questions. "*Are you and Lucas back together? Why are you hanging out with each other? Do you want to be back together?*"

Questions I didn't know how to answer.

"Besides, Blaire, it's only four. You really think Mom's shindig is going to run for much longer? Gram's probably going to start loading up the car soon."

There it was again. That familiarity. That hint that he knew me, my life, my family on a personal level. And he did. He'd been there for holidays and birthday parties.

Which made everything harder. "She's not your gram," I said with a serious tone, pushing off the counter. "Stop calling her that."

"It's a habit."

"Well, break it."

For a moment, we stared at each other, locked in competition. Whoever blinked first would be wrong.

It wasn't me, of course. He was the one in the wrong. He shouldn't be talking to Gram behind my back, trying to weasel his way into my life. The two of them had probably talked on the phone for hours and conspired about this very moment. Was that why Gram had asked me to come inside and make the lemonade? Why she'd made me redo my makeup this morning? I would've laid money on it. And all because Lucas had decided it'd be a good idea to try and win over my own grandmother.

But guess what, Lucas? She's loyal to me.

Despite my being right, though, I couldn't stop myself from reflexively blinking, silently declaring myself the star-ing-contest loser.

Lucas sat back in his seat, satisfied. "Are you planning on wearing that tonight?"

"My pretty, pretty princess outfit?"

"Oh, is that what you're dressed up as?"

I fought the urge to reach over and smack him. "I'd never go out in public in this thing." You know, if I wasn't getting paid for it.

Lucas rested both of his elbows onto the countertop, leaning forward until his head rested on the heels of his hands. Peering up at me through his lashes, he said, "Who said anything about going out in public?"

Six

"*Evil Killer Babies?*" I demanded, holding the DVD case in my hand. The cover art looked so cheap with a picture of a doodled baby on a plain red background. The baby's eyes, though, were entirely black, and its smile looked smeared with paint. Probably supposed to be blood, but the shade was way too bright. "What kind of stupidity is this?"

"Not stupidity," Donnie said as he ripped the case away. He was probably afraid I'd throw the DVD against the wall. "It's an art."

Lucas nodded from where he sat on the adjacent couch. We all sat downstairs in Donnie's finished basement, where the giant flat-screen was positioned against a concrete wall. The couches were well-loved and mismatched. Lucas sat on the red-and-blue plaid sofa, while I sat on the velvet green one. Perfect distance. "Yes, being such a tragically horrible movie is an art. I mean, it's a thousand-year-old baby who comes back from the dead to go on a killing spree. How epic is that?"

Yeah, *so* epic.

Donnie knelt in front of the DVD player, analyzing the cases. "We've got a good lineup. After *Evil Killer Babies,* we're going to watch *Zombears* and then *Nun Zombies* 2, because the second is way better than the first."

"What's with you guys and the undead? And are you sure we're going to get through everything in one night?" *Please say no.*

"Of course," Lucas said, all but scoffing. "We've had longer movie nights before."

Donnie slid the DVD into the player and pushed to his feet. "I'm going to go make popcorn. We still like extra butter, right?"

"Yes," Lucas and I answered at the same time.

Once Donnie headed upstairs, I couldn't ignore the strangeness that hung in the air. Meeting in Donnie's basement, binge-watching a few movies—it felt like old times. I never sat on this couch, though; I always sat on the plaid one with Lucas.

Donnie had a rule about not being too lovey-dovey in front of him, so we'd held hands under the blankets, using it to shield our lovey-dovey moments. Now, we sat separated, and my hands were planted firmly in my lap.

This couch was much lumpier than the plaid one.

I drew my knees up to my chest, my leggings stretching with the movement. I'd gone home halfway through helping Gram clean up her trays and lemonade pitchers to change, as per Lucas's order. Even though I'd hoped otherwise, Gram hadn't asked me to stay. "Oh, of course, Blaire, go," she'd said. "You haven't been out of the house in weeks. You need to live a little."

Yeah. Ouch.

"Did you ever read your dad's letter?"

I jerked at the suddenness of Lucas's voice, immediately thinking about the ugly orange envelope in my backpack. "Aren't you nosy?"

"Not nosy," Lucas said now, not even looking at me. He studied the trailers on the TV as if they genuinely interested him. "Just respectfully curious. You *did* flaunt it in my face the other day."

My jaw dropped. "I did not! You read it over my shoulder!"

"*Mmm*," was all that came from him, nearly drowned out by the music rising on the TV.

I settled back deeper into the sofa cushions. "I know what you're doing. You're pretending to be disinterested to get me to tell you. Reverse psychology doesn't work on me."

"I think you're overthinking this, Bee. I was only trying to make conversation."

Oh, yeah. Right. He'd been Nosy McNoserson the entire time, and he claimed that *now* he just was "making conversation"? Psh. I didn't buy it.

I let out a sharp sigh. "If you must know, I kept it, but I didn't read it. And I'm not going to. I can't even imagine opening it—the idea makes me sick. I don't need to hear you give me crap about not reading a letter from my dad, okay? Gram's got that base covered. Seriously."

Lucas watched me as I went on my small rant, eyes wide. "You sure are defensive, aren't you?"

I clenched my teeth together. "You know, I think I'm seeing too much of you. Two days in a row is too much."

Now his voice sounded amused. "You used to see me every day before."

Before, before, before.

Gah. Could Donnie take any longer? I folded my arms tight across my chest. "Can you be quiet? I'm trying to watch the trailers."

I wasn't. What I *was* trying to do, though, was effectively block him out. No boy sat on the ugly couch across the room, surely not a boy I'd kissed before. Definitely not an ex-boyfriend. Nope. Not there. The basement was empty, and I sat by myself, watching these crappy trailers.

Once upon a time, Lucas had known every little thing about me. He knew I wanted to open my own bakery one day and decorate cookies and cupcakes until my heart crapped out. He knew I preferred pickles on the side of my sandwiches rather than in it. He knew exactly how I liked my coffee.

Honestly, I wanted nothing more than to confide in him, to crack apart and tell him everything, but this was something about myself that I couldn't share.

"I can practically hear the hamster wheel in your brain whirling."

How long does it take to pop popcorn, Donnie?

A sigh came from the direction of the other couch. "Bee, I'm trying hard to understand you, but you've got to help me out here."

I was fully aware how childish I sounded when I spoke. "Oh, I've *got to*, huh?"

"One day, things between us are fine. More than fine—I mean, we almost—"

"Almost *nothing*," I cut him off sharply, still glaring at the TV screen. "I don't have to explain it to you."

"How would you feel if the tables were turned? How would you feel if, after a night like we spent together, I just broke up with you? No warning, no time to talk about it. That I told you 'I'm breaking up with you' and that was it?"

As he spoke, strong emotion filling his voice, my heart began to beat. Faster and faster until I thought I was going to throw up. When I was younger, I thought "I love you" was a feeling that lasted forever. That "I love you" meant "I would never leave you." That the phrase was a promise, one that could never be broken.

And listening to Lucas become as emotional as I'd ever seen him, I sat among the shards of that broken promise, shattered like glass.

"What does it matter *why*?" I asked, voice sounding almost silent compared to the roaring blood in my ears. "What does it matter when it changes *nothing*?"

"You know it matters, Bee."

Despite my better knowledge, I turned my head to look at him, the pain in my chest spreading everywhere. It wasn't my own selfish pain. Knowing I was putting

Lucas through all this *hurt*. It made everything so much worse.

Lucas's gaze remained steady, a pure wave of blue that lapped against white sand. I knew his eyes so well. I knew them well enough to know that when we kissed, they turned into a storm-cloud color, the hue of the sky before it began to rain. And when he grew tired, they practically glowed through his lidded lashes. They got that way when he got angry too. And they got that way when he felt sad.

So now, as I looked at him, his eyes glowing like electricity had been plugged into them, I had no idea what he was feeling—tired, angry, or sad.

"I didn't mean to hurt you," I told him honestly.

"But you did. And it's like you don't even care."

Denial rose in my throat, sharp and fierce, but the words never left my mouth. I *had* hurt him. I was still hurting him. Part of this was his fault. He'd pushed to do this friend thing, to do all these fall activities. Yeah, sure, I'd agreed to them, but he'd suggested it in the first place.

But going even earlier than that, the night in the car when I'd broken things off—that's what he meant. And that was 100% on me.

"I don't know what's changed for you," Lucas said, and he looked away from me, back to the trailers. "But nothing's changed for me."

They were the words I wanted to hear—words I'd been craving to hear—but my traitorous mind wouldn't believe them.

"Popcorn is done," Donnie announced, thundering down the stairs, oblivious to the weight that clung to the air. He came happily into the room, already munching on a handful of kernels. "I think I really made it to perfection this time."

"It's microwave popcorn." Lucas chuckled, taking his separate bowl from Donnie. His voice was completely unbothered. "There's not much to do other than press the start button."

Just like that, the conversation had been pushed aside. Unfinished. Ignored.

Donnie sat down next to me, fluffing the fuzzy blanket over my legs to make room.

"How is watching crappy movies in your damp basement supposed to get me to love Halloween?" I asked, begrudgingly grabbing some popcorn. My heart still beat fast, a hummingbird released in my ribcage, but at least the rushing of blood wasn't so loud in my ears anymore.

My voice, too, wasn't as chaotic as it had been. No, it was level now. Even. Unbothered.

"Scary movies are the epitome of the season," Donnie said, setting the bowl in the space between our legs. "We picked crappy ones because truly scary movies give Lucas nightmares."

Lucas's response came quick. "They do not."

I snorted before I could stop myself. "Did you forget what happened when we watched *The Mirror Man*? You made me video-chat you until you fell asleep."

He blinked a few times, probably trying to process the

change in our mood. "That—that was so not how it happened."

The night we'd watched that movie had been a while ago, before we'd officially started dating. That night had been like this one—in Donnie's basement, with Donnie and a bowl of popcorn between us. Lucas and I had been at that stage where we'd both been too afraid to look each other in the eye for longer than a few seconds, like if we looked too long, we'd spontaneously combust. As I'd laid down to go to sleep, I'd gotten a text from him. *Why do the shadows in my closet have faces? I need a distraction.*

And he'd video-chatted me, both of us in bed, until our eyes slipped low.

He'd fallen asleep first, lips parted as whatever he'd been saying had trailed off, breathing finally evening out. I could still remember the clear thought in my mind. *I'm going to love this boy forever.*

"Can we skip to the movie?" I demanded, shoving away the thoughts and memories. They weren't helpful. Not in the slightest. Grabbing a fistful of popcorn, I settled deeper into the hard couch, trying to ignore how much I wished I was on the plaid one. "Let's get this over with."

Seven

"*Y*ou look like a dork."

Donnie didn't even glance down at himself as I spoke to him, his expression self-assured. "I do not."

I pressed my lips tightly together to keep from smiling. "You definitely do. Why are you dressed like a *shark*?"

Or, at least, that's what I thought he was supposed to be. The silvery-blue material covered his entire body, accented with a hood and a face hole. It didn't quite reach his ankles, which made the whole thing look a little silly. An extra bunching of material gathered at his armpits, so his arms stuck out a little at his sides.

A tiny little fin was even attached to his back, and it flapped with each movement he made.

"It's sea-life dress-up day," Donnie said in a cheerful voice. "I thought this was pretty clever."

"Sea-life dress-up day? That's a *thing*?"

"It's spirit week. Remember? Everyone dresses in the

costume theme for the day. Monday is sea-life." Donnie wiggled his arms to punctuate his words.

I'd forgotten that during the week of Halloween, Hallow High hosted a spirit week. They should've put *that* poster on my locker. Not that I would've participated either way, but I would've been more prepared for the fish and squids roaming the halls. "And you found *this*?"

Donnie scowled at me, finally handing over my coffee. The costume didn't have any holes for hands, so he'd had to cup it with his blue fin. "I think my costume looks pretty good, thank you very much. Don't be a *jerk*-o-lantern."

"Oh my gosh, that was so *cringy*."

"Hey, I look better than Mike Apton in his stupid clownfish costume. He just painted orange stripes on his shirt. *Boooring*."

I smirked as I took my cup, bringing it to my nose to make sure he hadn't ruined this one too. The delightful bitterness greeted me, making me shiver. "Hey, I have some money for the coffee," I told him, reaching into my backpack. It hadn't occurred to me to start paying Donnie—I used to give Lucas money for them, but it had kind of slipped my mind to pay Donnie. Those lattes and espressos added up. I pulled out the small envelope I'd put it in, offering it out to him. "That should cover next month."

"Sorry, sharks don't have pockets," he said automatically.

"Seriously. Take it."

Donnie wiggled his fin. "I can't. No fingers. Can't grab."

"Fine." As quickly as I could manage, I shoved the envelope down the face hole of his costume, effectively getting it stuck inside his suit. "It's like one giant pocket."

"Aw, come on, Blaire. I'm going to have to take this thing off to get that."

A group of students hurried down the hallway, all in the same direction. They were dressed as some sort of sea creatures—fish, eels, different things. I caught a girl pulling her cell phone out of her pocket, quickly swiping to the camera mode.

"What's going on?" I asked Donnie, trying to see what they looked at. "School doesn't start for ten more minutes."

"The envelope is poking me in the stomach," he complained, as if he hadn't heard me. "What'd you go and put it in an envelope for, anyway? Only rich people buying people off do that. Envelopes are for hush money."

"You're *so* weird, Donnie. And you watch way too much TV."

The shark stuck his tongue out at me.

I sipped at my espresso, the taste coating my tongue and making it shrivel. Donnie said the bitterness in my coffee rubbed off on me, but I almost thought the opposite was true. Maybe my coffee kept my bitter personality at bay. All the anger and the negativity were held off by the amazingness of coffee. I could buy into that fact.

But my hypothesis proved false when I finally saw what all those students hurried toward, and a huge wave of resentment hit me at once. And pain. Lots of that.

"And you thought *my* costume was bad," Donnie said

from beside me, pulling his pumpkin-spice nonsense to his lips.

If things were different, I would've burst out laughing. I would've had to press a hand over my mouth to keep from full-on ugly cackling, because *this* was a sight to see.

Lucas walked down the hallway clad in a green-and-teal mermaid tail and a bright coral seashell bra. He had on a white t-shirt underneath his bra, but it only made the vibrant color pop more. He'd dampened his hair down to sweep across his forehead, and even from here, it looked dripping wet.

All in all, he looked ridiculous. Worse than Donnie, for sure. But that wasn't what made my insides tie in angry, aching knots.

Hailey Moore walked beside him, in a mermaid tail and seashell bra of her own. Her blonde hair flowed over her shoulders in beautiful waves, and her makeup had contours of pink and purple, blended out perfectly.

Of course, she looked beautiful.

They weren't holding hands or even touching, but in my mind, they might as well have had their arms wrapped around each other. Everything was perfectly clear. *They planned this.*

"It could've been an accident," Donnie said from beside me, easily reading my thoughts. His voice sounded tentative, his expression probably anxious. There would've been a tightness to his eyes, his teeth worrying at his lip. "Like, they both showed up as the same thing?"

It would've been a good argument if their seashell bras weren't the same color and their tails didn't match.

"It doesn't matter," I said instead, taking a sip of my coffee. I let it fill my mouth, burning my taste buds. "It's good that she's doing it with him—no way would I have dressed up like a fish."

Donnie choked on his pumpkin-spice garbage. "Too bad. What a great Christmas card that would've been."

In that moment, I was the one who felt like a dork in that hallway. The only one not wearing a costume, watching my ex and his ex walk down the hallway with matching outfits. And they couldn't have dressed as anything ugly, like a stonefish—no, they had to be *mermaids*, which were beautiful and unique. So not fair.

I wanted to break something.

This time, when Lucas walked past, he never even glanced my way.

I wanted this, didn't I? Space? So why did it feel as if someone had reached inside and ripped my lungs into shreds?

"Blaire?" Donnie laid a fin on my shoulder. "Are you okay?"

I shrugged it off, slamming my locker shut. "Let's go to class."

"But your coffee—"

As I headed in the opposite direction Lucas and Hailey had gone, I tipped my coffee cup high, filling my mouth with the blistering liquid. Neither the heat nor the bitterness chased the feeling away. The empty cup rattled in my grip as I lowered it, dumping it in a nearby trash can. "All gone," I told him, knowing I'd be jittery for the rest of the day.

Classes passed slowly. I had to suffer through stupid ocean puns—"*Shell* we go over our homework?" and "*Seas* the day, kids!" and "Who's feeling *fin*-tastic today?"—and I was about ready to smack anyone who spoke to me. I'd have to endure a whole week of this nonsense. Dressing up, stupid puns. It was going to be a rough week.

As the day went on, I got to see that many people had the wise ideas to dress up as mermaids, which only served as a potent reminder of this morning. Would Lucas and Hailey match every day of costume week? Were they going to the Halloween Bash together?

Something inside me went very still very fast. For high schoolers, the Halloween Boo-Bash was considered to be bigger than the homecoming dance. Would Lucas and Hailey dress up together?

I pulled my backpack over my shoulder and brought it around to my chest, peeking inside to find Dad's orange letter winking at me. Inexplicably, looking at the thing made me it easier to breathe. Like I could remember more important things existed than Lucas and Hailey and stupid Halloween parties and princess costumes.

I reached in and ran my fingertip along the front of it, tracing the blocky black penmanship.

Ridiculous. After zipping my backpack shut, I slung it

over my shoulder, heading for the double doors. Tomorrow was "dress like your favorite celebrity" day, so that would be *the best*. I'd be trading in *shell yeahs* for stupid celebrity catchphrases and TV show quotes. *Maybe I'll call in sick. Yeah, Gram, I'm not feeling too well.*

"You ready for your next October activity?" Without warning, Lucas saddled up next to me, a textbook in his hand, jacket in the other. His mermaid tail swooshed against the linoleum floors as we walked, his steps more of a shuffle. "It's going to be fun."

"Oh, we're still doing that?" I asked, unable to look at him. "I would've thought after our scary movie nightmare, we'd throw in the towel."

"You agreed to four outings," Lucas said, stepping ahead of me to open one of the doors. He moved unthinkingly, out of habit, holding it out so I could pass through. "We still have three more. Now, I know you're a quitter, but I'm not."

I sucked in a sharp breath, the blow low enough to hurt. He'd spoken in a lighthearted tone, but it still stung.

Squaring my shoulders, I walked past him into the chilly October air. A bright coral color burned the corner of my eye. "I can't take you seriously with that thing on."

He readjusted his seashell bra. "It's cute, right? It goes with my complexion."

"And Hailey's."

Our eyes met. I would've thought his expression might look smug, teasing. A *"you're jealous, aren't you?"* comment coming from his mouth.

But he didn't look smug. A beat of silence passed, and I would've given anything in the world to know what he was thinking. Did he draw out the silence to make me squirm? Was he thinking about Hailey and her seashell bra? Did he know I was jealous?

"Can I give you a ride home?" Those blue eyes traced my face gently, like a caress of a fingertip.

"I'd rather walk." I wasn't sure if that was the truth or yet another lie. They were stacking up lately.

But if my answer disappointed Lucas, he didn't show it. "I already checked with Donnie, and he said he's up for tonight. I'll swing by your place at six?"

"Wait, tonight? Jeez, will you ever give me notice?"

"I like to keep you on your toes," he said with a wink, one that practically flashed through me.

Goosebumps swept over my skin as a breeze passed between us, pulling at my hair and winding it around my face. I batted at it, tucking it behind my ears, and for a brief moment, I fantasized about the idea of Lucas reaching out. He'd push my hair back himself, his skin grazing my cheeks in the process. He used to do that when he wanted to look into my eyes, to see right through me.

Lucas shuddered as the breeze caught at his bare arms, but that was his only reaction. His free hand tightened into a fist. "So, tonight works?"

"I'll have to check with Gram," I said, using my one last possible excuse, but we both knew what she'd say.

. . .

"Of course you can go out tonight," Gram assured when I asked, tucking a hanger of *something* into the racks of costumes. It was black, that much I could see, but I couldn't remember if we had any black costumes. She'd been messing with a scrap of black fabric the other day, the more I thought about it. Probably something she was working on for a new party. "You don't have to ask me for permission, Blaire. I trust you."

I slumped into the chair in the corner of the room, sighing. Yeah, stupid of me to hold out hope that she'd have a different answer, but that was the last card I could play. "You shouldn't trust me. I make dumb decisions."

"All teenagers make dumb decisions," Aunt Aimee said with a high laugh, bent over the sewing machine with her fingers pressed against a strip of fabric. She'd greeted me with a smile when I came into the room, her interest piqued now. "It's allowed when you're young."

I'd always thought Aunt Aimee looked more like Mom than Dad, who was her biological brother. Aimee's hair was practically the same color as Mom's—a nearly brown blonde—and they even used to have it cut the same. Both tall, slender. Seeing Aunt Aimee used to open up a rift in my stomach, especially when everything had been fresh. She'd reminded me too much of Mom.

Now, looking at her only made my heart pinch a little.

"Don't listen to her." Gram sighed, waving a hand. "Name one dumb decision you've made in your life, Blaire."

"I pour the milk in before the cereal. People think that's

weird."

"Blaire." Gram turned to face me fully, and the long skirt she wore belled out with the movement. She placed her hands on her hips, giving me her best parental stare. "You've never given me a reason not to trust you. Lucas and Donnie haven't, either."

Aunt Aimee stepped on the pedal of the sewing machine, bringing it to life. "I'd trust those two with my life."

I narrowed my eyes at her because she *so* wasn't helping. "I don't even know what we're doing. Surely you can't let me out of the house not knowing where I'm going to be."

Gram frowned a little. "Do you want to tell me what this is about?"

What a loaded question. I wished she could read my mind so I wouldn't have to say anything aloud. I wouldn't have to tell her about my breakup. I wouldn't have to tell her how much Dad's letter upset me. I wouldn't have to tell her how I was so full of negativity lately that I couldn't recognize who I was turning into.

My eyes glanced past her to Aunt Aimee, who tried to pretend like she wasn't listening. "This isn't about anything."

With only two years of reading my cues, Gram was left at a disadvantage. We'd visited her house often when Mom had been alive and Dad around, but not well enough for her to read and recognize each of my idiosyncrasies. Like now, as I pulled at my shirt sleeves, covering my fingers, Mom would've recognized that something was up.

But Gram, still new at this, didn't realize, and the gesture went over her head. "If you're sure," she said, gaze lingering in case I caved and spilled my guts.

"I meant to ask you the other day—Delia, Lucas's little sister, is looking for accessories for her Halloween costume. Do you think she could come over and pick through what we've got? I think it might be fun for her."

Delia had asked about it again at her mom's tea party, when she'd shown me her bedroom. More specifically, she'd shown me the paint on the walls, a light lilac color. She'd been quite proud to have the pink gone, since purple was "much more grown-up."

"That does sound fun," Gram said, glancing at the table full of jewelry she had pressed against the far wall. A trunk sat right next to it with other odds and ends. "If she promises to return everything, I don't see the harm."

"Maybe you can pawn your glass shoes off on her, Blaire," Aunt Aimee said with a wink, straightening out the piece of fabric in front of her.

"Don't encourage her, Aimee," Gram scolded, coming over and reaching out her hand. "Now let's go make a snack before you have to leave, yeah?"

I found my eyes trailing back to the closet, to the black scrap of fabric Gram had tried to tuck in between the other garments. It stuck out like a sore thumb, a dark color among mostly light fabrics. Though I wanted to, I didn't ask about it. I found myself grabbing hold of her small hand instead, allowing her to pull me to my feet.

eight

I shuddered deep in my jacket as I stepped out of the small car, taking in the sight before me. For the first time since the start of all this Halloween nonsense, I actually felt *excited*.

I know. Scary.

Lucas had driven to the next town over, to Addison, and parked in front of Albion Family's Corn Maze and Hayrides. For a Monday night, there were a lot of people. Families stood in line for hayrides or headed into the corn mazes. The farm even had an area where someone could buy pumpkins, and children wandered through the rows of them, trying to find the perfect one. I couldn't help but smile.

This wasn't me relenting to the spirit of Halloween. I refused.

Lucas's boots crunched over the stones in the parking lot as he rounded the car, eyes darting between Donnie and me. "Who's ready to hang with the scarecrows?"

"You mean get *eaten* by scarecrows?" Donnie's eyes widened. "I've seen that horror movie."

I gave him a serious look. "I'm definitely tripping you to live."

"I'll get a map in case we get lost," Lucas said, patting Donnie's shoulder as he brushed past. "No scarecrow-eating going on in our group."

Donnie's arm stiffened as I looped mine through it, tugging him after Lucas. "You're going to trip *him* first, right?" Donnie asked me, voice lowered.

I watched Lucas continue toward the map booth, his stride even and relaxed. He walked several paces ahead of us, almost as if he'd come to the corn maze alone. "Oh, totally. I mean, the ex always goes first. Never the quirky supporting character."

"Hey, I'm only a supporting character?"

I snorted, tossing my hair back in a dramatic fashion. "Well, you're not the *star*."

Donnie hip-checked me, but since I was still latched onto his arm, we both stumbled together.

"Besides, Lucas is the one who's supposed to be scared of horror movies," I told him. "What's up with you being afraid of scarecrows?"

"Uh, have you *seen* that movie where the scarecrow eats people? And eats the one kid's *eyes*?" Donnie shuddered, whether from the cold or from the idea of getting his eyes eaten, I wasn't sure. "It scarred me for life."

"Maybe if we find a scarecrow, you can take a picture with it. Get over your fear. Before it eats you, I mean."

He glared at me. "Not helpful." Despite his serious tone, he didn't let go of my arm. He puffed out a breath, which clouded in the air. "It's cold tonight. I wonder how cold it's going to be on Saturday."

"Trying to plan out your Boo-Bash costume?" I couldn't remember if he'd ever decided what he planned on going as.

"Of course."

Lucas glanced back at us as he stepped up to the booth, hands in his jacket's pockets. One dark eyebrow arched. "Are you guys coming?"

I hadn't been to a corn maze in years. It'd been eighth grade, and I'd gone with Mom and Dad. We definitely hadn't come here, because none of this looked familiar, but whichever corn maze we'd gone to sucked. The corn hadn't grown tall, and if Dad had stood on his tiptoes, he could've seen through the wisps of the corn to the exit. He'd let me work my way through it, of course, and hadn't cheated, but we'd ended up finishing in a matter of minutes.

I'd been bummed by how lame it'd been, but Mom— ever and always the optimist—had said the time we'd spent together made it worth it.

Yeah...looking back, I'd definitely agree.

"Welcome to Albion Family Farms," the girl at the booth said as we approached, her smile blinding in the dark. She looked about our age, soft eyes glancing between all of us. "Are you here for the corn maze or hayride?"

"The maze," Lucas answered politely.

"For the three of you, that'll be fifteen dollars." She

popped open the metal box in front of her. "We have an easy, medium, and hard course—they're all marked at the entrance."

After Lucas passed over three bills, we made our way over to the maze entrances, and I gave him a cool look. "You didn't say this would cost money. I would've brought some."

"We talked you into doing this, Bee. That would've been lame if I expected you to pay."

"I wouldn't have minded."

Donnie turned the map over in his hands. He'd swiped it up as we passed the booth, but hadn't opened it yet. "Are we doing the easy course?"

I drew my arm from him, rubbing my hands together in anticipation. "Psh, easy? You can. I, for one, am going all in."

Lucas's expression didn't change, but Donnie's lips pulled downward. Even more so at my next suggestion.

"*And* I say we should go without a map," I went on, glancing at the paper Donnie clutched like a lifeline. "Have some fun with it. Get lost and have a whole search party try to find us."

"That *does* sound like a fun time," Lucas said with an eye roll, but as he slipped his hands into his pockets, he had a hint of a smile.

Donnie shot us both a glare. "I disagree. If we're going the hard way, we're taking a map."

Lucas glanced up at the sky. "Whatever we're doing, let's go before we lose our daylight."

He was right. Sunlight was disappearing fast. The sunset stopped looking orangey-yellow and now clung to a purply-blue color. All the colors blended like a mix of paints, speckled with stars trying to prematurely poke their way through. Nights came early now that fall was in full swing, along with chilly breezes. I huddled deeper into my jacket, flipping up the collar as high as it would go, wishing I'd brought along something warmer.

"What made you think of a corn maze for a Halloween festivity?" I asked the boys as we walked through the maze arch, reading the sign: WARNING: *Hard course ahead. Enter at your own risk.* Dramatic much? "I never would've thought of this."

"It's a classic fall activity," Lucas said, glancing over his shoulder in my direction. "This was my idea, by the way. We had two ideas each."

"Scary movies were my idea," Donnie added. "But the next two are top secret."

Top secret. Yeah, I'd have bet money on the fact that pumpkin carving had made the list, but I wasn't sure who would've picked it. Probably Donnie.

The corn shifted as the October breeze cut across the tops, the husks rustling together noisily. Run-down stalks crushed against the ground, and we walked on top of them, finding our way through. It almost looked like a horror movie, with the darkening sky and the crackling sound. The only difference, though, was the fact that I could still hear laughter from other groups of people wandering through the mazes, even children's giggles.

We walked in relative silence. Here and there, we'd discuss which way to turn, but otherwise, only the sound was the crunching of cornstalks under our shoes. After a while, Lucas walked a pace or two ahead of Donnie and me, the aisle not wide enough for the three of us to walk side by side.

Stiffness clung to Lucas's shoulders, pulling his jacket taut.

If Donnie noticed something off in the air, he didn't say anything. Then again, this must've seemed like the new normal. Totally opposite of how things used to be. We were always talking, always laughing. Now, there was silence.

To make matters worse, it started to rain.

Well, not *rain*. More of a sprinkle, but a cold one, and my shivering worsened.

Lucas stopped walking, letting out a sigh.

"What's wrong?" Donnie asked.

"It's a dead end."

I looked around the curve of his shoulder to find an abrupt wall of corn. I swiped a raindrop from my eye. "Another one?"

Lucas turned around. His hair had begun to dampen, curling at the ends. Donnie's had already full-on frizzed. "Let's backtrack."

This was the fifth dead end we'd walked into, but they branched off each other. We'd been walking in the same direction for a while.

Donnie left his map in his back pocket, keeping the spirit alive, but my fingers started to go numb. "I don't even remember which direction we came from," I muttered as we finally came back to a crossroads, three separate paths stretched out ahead of us.

"We came from that one." Donnie pointed to the left. "I remember because I tripped over that piece of corn. Wait, or was it *that* piece of corn..."

"So if we came from the left, we should go straight," I said, peering down the trail. It looked dark and quiet, as if no one was down there. "Or go right. Which one?"

Not many people were in this maze with us, families no doubt choosing the easier mazes. They'd probably had the right idea. I guess that ominous sign at the entrance knew what it was talking about.

"Let's go straight," Lucas said from behind me, stepping over fallen corn stalks. "We've barely started. Surely we can't be *that* lost."

"Didn't we already try to go that way earlier?" Donnie leaned down the straight corn aisle and glanced around. "I think we tried to go through that one and we hit a dead end."

"I'll check out the straight path," I told them, shoving forward. "You two head right. If I'm wrong, I'll come find you. If you're wrong, come find me."

Donnie's response came immediately. "This is a bad, bad idea. This is what happens in scary movies when people split up. Going off by yourself ensures your grue-some demise by murderous scarecrows."

"You're super dramatic, you know that?" I turned around and smiled as I moved down the branch of the maze. Both boys watched me go, but I forced myself to focus on Donnie. "You should've taken theater."

The sky had darkened considerably since we'd gotten to the maze, but for almost seven-thirty at night, it made sense. A chunk of a moon hung in the sky, not quite full, but it did have a haze over it, the misty rain like a shrugged-on coat.

Corn stalks shuffled loudly in the wind, and I wrapped my arms around myself, keeping my eyes ahead. *Murderous scarecrows.* Donnie needed to lay off the horror flicks. *Evil Killer Babies* had totally left his brain cells fried. There was no way a scarecrow was going to come off its post and eat us. They had straw for arms—there's no strength in straw.

Great. Now *I* was thinking about it.

I stomped further down the vacant path, flinching as a rain droplet fell onto my lashes. We should've gone on the hayride. I'd never been on a hayride before. It would've been fun, right?

Then again, the three of us probably would've been silent the whole time too, only trapped on a trailer.

Would've been better than this, going through a corn maze on my own, picturing my death by a freaking scarecrow.

Being away from Lucas helped clear my mind a little, but it also made me feel emptier, as silly as that sounded. I didn't need a guy to make me whole, but was it bad that I craved his presence? Because now, even though we had been silent and the air had been tense, I just wished he was here walking with me.

A fat droplet of rain landed on my cheek, much more substantial than the mist that coated me, and the fear of the sky suddenly cracking open became more of a reality. The sides of the corn seemed to be pressing in, and for a split second, I entertained the idea of cutting through them. Surely the maze would intersect *somewhere*.

Something snapped behind me, sounding exactly like the breaking of a bone. When I whirled around, a scream already lodging in my throat, I saw it wasn't a scarecrow.

It was Lucas, his black sneaker on top of a turned-over cornstalk. He froze. "Hey."

"Why are you following me?" I demanded, pulling my arms closer around myself. "Did Donnie send you?"

"More or less. We were both worried about you getting—"

"I'm not going to get eaten by a scarecrow!" I cut him off so loudly that my voice echoed.

Lucas's eyes widened. "I was going to say *getting lost*, but all right."

My cheeks turned hot. Okay, fine, getting lost might've been a more appropriate fear. Especially when I was over here thinking about cutting through the thick cornfield to find a different path.

"Well, let's keep going," I said, turning away from him. Now it was my turn to have stiff shoulders, since I could practically feel his gaze on my back. "I think Donnie was wrong. I don't think we've been down here. This curve looks different to me—I don't remember rounding it."

"It's corn in the dark. How can you tell it's different?"

I couldn't; I'd only tried to make conversation. No idea why. Maybe because I hated the tension between us, like a thick second skin. I kicked a fallen piece of corn and walked further, not answering.

For some reason, this moment made me recall our first and only fight as a couple. It hadn't been a fight so much as a disagreement, over something I couldn't even remember, but our mutual cold shoulders had lasted for a whole day, even through school.

However, just because we'd disagreed over something, things between us hadn't been that different. Lucas had still stopped by the apartment to drive me to school, still swung through Crushed Beanz and picked us up coffee, still walked me to my first period class. And I'd still bought him an extra cookie at lunch, hung out by his locker during the break between fourth and fifth period, still let him steal a piece of gum at the end of the day.

We'd done all those things silently, but not out of habit. Not because we had to, but because we hadn't wanted to *not* do it. I hadn't wanted to *not* buy him his cookie, and he hadn't wanted to *not* walk me to homeroom. Even though we'd been fighting, we'd still cared.

Right now, it didn't feel like that at all.

After another minute of walking the curving path, I pulled up short as a firm wall of corn met me. Dead end. "Dang it," I muttered. "Donnie *was* right." Now I wasn't going to hear the end of it.

I turned around to start back when I smacked into Lucas, who'd stepped directly behind me. His jacket felt cold when I put my hands out, the smooth black material chilled in the night air.

We hadn't been this close since the night before our breakup, with our chests nearly touching now. It felt like it'd been forever since we shared the same breath. Forever since our body heat had mixed together, thawing some of the frost in my core. The heady warmth did something strange to my lungs now, my world turning and spinning beneath my feet.

I swallowed hard. "Why were you standing so close?"

"You're the one who stopped."

"You could've backed up." Or pulled away, which he still hadn't done. Then again, I hadn't moved away, either.

Lucas didn't say anything, and I didn't look up to see the expression on his face.

My hands on his jacket sleeves, what originally had been a grip to steady myself, now turned into me not letting go. And I needed to let go, but I couldn't pry my ten fingers apart.

The night of our breakup had been so final. Except standing here with our chests almost touching and our breath mixing, it didn't seem final at all.

One of Lucas's fingertips brushed the curve of my cheek, an icy touch against my blushing skin. That whisper of contact alone made me shiver harder than the October air made me, and I fought it back, not wanting him to see.

"Your skin is cold," he murmured, that low voice cascading through me.

My eyes focused on the silver zipper of his jacket, the metal looking like crooked teeth. "I wonder why."

"So much snark." He shook his head, his finger trailing lower, along my jaw. "But you can't fool me."

Couldn't I? Honestly, I wasn't even sure I was fooling myself anymore. I wanted two completely opposite things— I wanted him closer, and I wanted him away.

He had all the warmth with him, and I wanted it. I craved to dive deep into it. If his arms wrapped around me in a way they hadn't in a while, I wouldn't have fought it. His jacket would crinkle in my ear, and I'd tip my head up to look at him, into those beautiful blue eyes—

With a sharp inhale, I pulled back, dropping my arms and stepping away from his outstretched hand. Heat swamped my skin, no doubt turning my face tomato-red. No way would I look at him. "Come on, we should find Donnie before he gets too far ahead."

Donnie would separate this tension. Donnie would clear my foggy thoughts. He'd say something silly about murderous scarecrows, and we'd laugh and never speak of this again.

I'd only taken a few steps back down the way we came until I realized Lucas hadn't followed me; there were no trailing footsteps.

"Hailey asked me to the Halloween Bash."

Everything in me tensed as dread punched its way through my stomach. I whirled around to find Lucas not even two feet from me. A part of me hoped he'd only said what he had to get me to face him, but he looked dead serious. "W-What?"

"She texted me yesterday asking if I'd go with her to the Halloween store to pick out her outfits for this week." He took a step closer; only a foot of distance lingered between us now. "That's when we planned our mermaid costume. While we were at the store, she asked me."

My lips parted ever so slightly, but no words came out. Raindrops fell harder now, pasting my hair to my skin. Distantly, I could hear faint laughing, chattering conversations that sounded nothing like this one. It felt as if I was breathing underwater. "What did you tell her?"

His lips were pressed into a tight line, but his eyes glowed with emotion. *Angry, sad, or tired—what is he feeling?*

"No, don't tell me." I lifted my hand as if to cover his mouth, but I hovered an inch away. "You should go with her. I mean, she matched her bra with yours. *Totes* romantic."

"Your sarcasm is noted," Lucas replied carefully, annoyance crossing his gaze, "but—"

Now I did put my hand over his mouth. "No buts. Seriously. Go with her. You two were really cute together—now that you're single again, I say go for it."

I hate, hate, hated myself in that moment, because in my effort to be biting, I also became completely transparent.

Lucas reached up and pulled my hand away, fingers warm against my skin. The wind tugged at the dark, damp wisps cutting across his forehead. No divot dented his bottom lip now, no indent above the corner of his mouth. No trace of a smile in sight. "Maybe I will, Blaire."

"Good. There's absolutely no reason to tell her no." I curled my hand into a fist, trying to ignore the ghost pressure of his mouth against my palm. "We should go find Donnie."

More words lingered on the tip of my tongue, but I turned on my heel and practically ran away. The world weighed heavier and heavier with each step I took, because I was lying through my teeth, like a coward.

There *was* a reason to tell Hailey no, not that I could ever say that to him. I'd made my bed in this situation, and now it was time for a long, long sleep.

nine

"I think I'm going to be a princess instead of an old person." Delia twirled in front of the floor-length mirror, the excess fabric of the dress belling out with the movement. She wore one of Gram's extra princess costumes, an old one of mine that I'd outgrown. It was still big on her, way too long, but she'd wanted to try it on so badly. "Can I be a princess, Blaire?"

I sat on the floor on the opposite side of the wall, a book from English class open in my lap. For the longest time, Delia had sorted through the entire closet and the costume trunk, talking to herself, so I'd pulled out some homework to distract myself with.

With my thumb, I bookmarked the page. "You can be whatever you want, Delia. I just thought you and your friend were going as old people."

"Maybe he can be a prince instead. Or a frog."

"Definitely a frog. You don't need a prince." Talking

about princes made me think back to last night at the corn maze. After finding Donnie, we'd pretended like our whole almost-kissing/Halloween Bash conversation had never even happened.

On the drive home, Lucas mentioned that Delia had been asking when she could come over to the apartment to pick out a costume. It made me smile to think she really wanted to come, so after clearing it with Mrs. Avery— which had taken me forever to gather the courage to make the phone call—I'd swung by Delia's classroom after school, and we'd walked home together.

Delia now twirled again in front of the mirror, pulling at the sides of the dress. "It's a little big on me."

I set my book down on the ground and edged toward her. "Come here, I'll show you a trade secret."

The dress had been made for someone older, with hips and curves, so it swamped her. The top fit Delia all right—a little baggy in the front, but the width of her shoulders held the straps well. Only the length needed help. I reached under the tulle and grabbed a good amount of excess in my hands, folding it the way Gram taught me.

"You're not going to cut it, are you?" she asked worriedly, watching my movements.

"Nope. Folding it like this underneath the dress shortens the hemline a little bit," I told her, and once I was sure I had the fabric entirely in my one hand, I reached toward Gram's desk. "All we have to do is pin it in place."

When Costume Catering had first started, we hadn't

had much in the way of costumes. Gram had a thing against going to stores and buying something from a package. "Anyone can do that," she'd said. "I want us to be *unique*. I want to piece these costumes together myself."

So we'd gone to vintage thrift stores, but most of the pieces had been so worn or so ordinary that none of them had worked. The first piece of clothing Gram had found was this princess gown. It'd needed a massive workover, though. The fabric now was a pale lilac color, but before, it'd been a dirty sort of red. Gram had completely sewn together new fabric, added more tulle, altered the bodice. A total makeover for this one gown.

Our collection of costumes had quickly grown from there—we'd gone to antique shows, costume events, things like that—and so had our catering career.

Delia gasped a little as she looked in the mirror. "It doesn't even look like you pinned it!"

"Since I pinned it underneath the top layer, it kind of hides it," I told her, fluffing up the tulle and sitting back on my heels. "You're going to blow all those other princesses out of the water."

Delia's lips curved into a smile at that as she twisted and turned in front of the mirror, tipping her head back and forth. "I've missed this."

"Missed what?"

Those blue eyes met mine in the reflection. "Hanging out with you. I've missed you."

My heart constricted tightly in my chest.

I looked at her in the mirror, at the darkness of her hair tumbling over the dress, trapped in a moment in time. In the memory of a time where I could still fit into this dress, of how it had looked to have my hair falling down the back of it. This dress was worse than the blue one because it was the first time I'd had to settle into the role of a princess. I'd felt like I was trying to pull the wool over people's eyes. Trying to be a princess, beautiful and perfect, when I wasn't—not by a long shot.

"Well, you could be on our costume team, sweetheart!" Aunt Aimee said as she stepped into the doorway, folding her arms. "We might have to hire you."

That made Delia's smile reappear. "It was a little long, but Blaire shortened the bottom, so I won't trip."

"Oh!" Gram moved into view behind Aunt Aimee, laying a hand on her shoulder. "It looks so beautiful on you, Delia. You must keep it." She came into the room to peer at the gown further. I almost expected her to re-pin the dress, sure I'd done it wrong, but Gram seemed satisfied by my handiwork. "It doesn't fit anyone around here anymore."

Delia bent down and wrapped her arms around my neck, holding me tight. The dress crushed between us. "I'm so glad you're back, Blaire."

I sucked in a breath, my forehead crumpling as my brows drew together. Back in her life. Back in the Averys' lives. Back to being her friend.

But I wasn't back. In fact, after she left today, I had no idea when the next time I'd see her would be.

"Delia, your Mom's here," Aunt Aimee said, cutting into my thoughts. "We'll have to show her this dress, huh?"

Delia rolled her eyes as she pulled away from me, picking up her backpack from the corner of the room. "Mom'll probably say I've got too many dresses."

"She won't be able to say no to this one."

I climbed to my feet, leaving my book on the ground, but Delia was already heading out of the room. She turned around and waved goodbye before Aunt Aimee steered her in the direction of the stairwell. Before I could follow them, I noticed Gram standing still in the room, twisting her wedding ring around on her finger.

"Are you sure about giving her that dress?" I asked, worried about her fidgeting. "I know it was our first. I'm sure Delia won't mind. She has so many dresses."

"Oh, I'm not that sentimental, dear. It looked adorable on her. She can grow into it too. It's not that."

I reached out and placed my hand over hers, forcing her fingers to still. "Are you worrying about the Halloween Bash?" Officially four days until Halloween. Too early to do any real preparing for it, but not too early to begin stressing. Gram had been working with Aunt Aimee and Uncle John for the past few days now, checking and rechecking their ingredient inventory to make sure they'd have enough supplies. "It'll go great, Gram. I'll be a princess, Aunt Aimee will wear her totally not-age-appropriate nurse costume, you'll be...whatever you want to be, and it'll be great."

She swatted at me like she normally would, though the spark of wariness didn't leave her gaze. Gram stood several inches shorter than me—honestly, it was a feat for me to meet anyone who wasn't shorter than me—causing her to crane her neck to look into my eyes. I could clear as day see my father's gaze in hers, both of them sharing the same hazel hue. "How have you been lately, Blaire? Donnie's been saying that you don't seem like yourself."

Immediately, my guard flew up. I could definitely see Donnie sitting them down, trying to plan out an intervention. "I've been fine. Why?"

"We haven't talked about your father's letter."

I looked over her shoulder to the open closet, where a variety of colors and fabrics were about to spill out. A snippet of black caught my eye. "The one I asked you to throw away and you put it in my backpack?"

Gram was shameless. "That's the one."

"Talking about it won't change my mind," I told her, my insides starting to hum with frustration. "I'm not opening it. I'm not forgiving him."

"Opening the letter doesn't mean you're automatically forgiving him, Blaire."

Didn't it? Opening the letter was admitting defeat. It wasn't just opening a seal—it was opening a door, one that'd inevitably allow him to walk back into my life again. I knew me. If I let myself read that letter, I'd start to miss him, and that wasn't a road I could go down.

At least, not if I ever wanted to reverse off of it.

Gram reached out and pushed my hair from my face in a way that surprised me, rendering me still. The action was so *Dad*, flipping all my hair over my shoulder and reaching a hand up to touch my cheek. Her fingers were a little calloused from all the sewing she'd done over the years, but still gentle. "You'll do the right thing," she said softly. "No matter what you decide, I love you."

And with that, she walked out of the costume room.

The walls narrowed around me, like a prison's walls. *You'll do the right thing.* Definitely emotional manipulation. And come on, "the right thing"? Right thing by *her* standards, she meant. What about *me*? What about the right thing in my book?

I pressed both of my hands to my eyes, digging my fingers in until I saw stars. Unease crawled underneath my skin, swirling and slithering around like a snake.

Sometimes I forgot Gram was Dad's mom. I mean, I *knew* it, but I never *thought* about it. The fact sat there in the corner of my mind. I never thought about how Dad had left her too. What must it have been like for her, losing a daughter-in-law and her son leaving shortly after? She'd never spoken about it with me, probably afraid it'd shatter any sanity I'd managed to find after that horrible time in my life. I'd never asked her how it felt, how *she* felt.

I'd never asked her if Dad had sent her a letter too.

Slowly, I sank to the floor, leaning against the wall and drawing in a breath that almost burned. *It's not a big deal*, I tried to tell myself, over and over again until the words sounded like gibberish. *He left you. He's gone. Don't think about it. Get over it. Get over it.*

And I repeated that phrase, over and over in my head, until the burn in my throat faded away.

"Are you even *trying?*" Donnie demanded as he held onto the other end of the pumpkin, struggling with the weight. "And here I thought you had muscles."

I let out a puff of breath, trying not to cringe as the dirt from the pumpkin smeared across my chest. And of course, I'd decided to wear a white shirt on the day Donnie had wanted to go to the muddy pumpkin patch. We'd gone back to Albion Family's Corn Maze and Hayrides after school to pick out a few pumpkins, and had packed them into the back of Donnie's car. They'd bounced and rolled around the entire ride home.

Whereas I'd picked out a normal-sized pumpkin—one I could carry by myself with only a little bit of strain— Donnie had decided to pick out one that had required him and a buff farmhand to carry to the car. The only problem was now that he had no buff farmhand's help.

"*You're* the one who wanted the big one," I got out, my fingers slipping along the smooth surface. "Where's Lucas? He should be here to help you pick it up."

"Said he wanted to sit this one out."

I pretended not to know why, but I wasn't sure if my expression remained neutral.

We shuffled along the grass until we made it to

Donnie's back porch, and I hurried to put my end of the pumpkin down, my arms screaming with the effort. "I should've made you carve it in your trunk."

Donnie rubbed his dirty palms together, smacking away the loose dirt and grime. He also managed to get a smudge on his cheek—no idea how. "We did it, against all odds."

I crossed my arms over my chest, watching as he went back to the car and grabbed the carving supplies we'd bought from the farm. They were cheap plastic tools, but they'd get the job done. "Do you know why Lucas didn't come with us?"

You shouldn't care why, my brain whispered. *It doesn't matter, does it? It shouldn't.*

Right. It very much shouldn't, but I'd already asked.

"Blaire." Donnie sighed, holding a plastic pumpkin scooper out to me. "Do you want to talk about Lucas, or don't you? I can't keep up."

"I'm allowed to make conversation."

"Are you, though? Making conversation? Or are you prying?"

I gritted my teeth at him calling me out, kneeling in front of my pumpkin and using the sleeve of my jacket to wipe away most of the soil. Some of the other pumpkins had been washed clean and had looked pretty, but I'd chosen this one—a little lumpy and bumpy, a little dented and bruised. "Just forget it."

Donnie set a bucket up between the two of us for the

guts and then another for the seeds. "Lucas asked me to collect them," he told me, sitting back on his heels.

I pushed my sleeves up, holding my knife in a fist. "Do you know what you're going to carve?"

"I was just going to do a face."

I took in the surface of my pumpkin, a blank canvas, trying to imagine what could be carved there. It was a lot like a cookie or a cupcake that needed decorating, but carving it out instead of adding to it.

I had to put all my weight into cutting a shape at the top of my pumpkin, twisting the stem to pull off the lid. It made a crackling noise, stringing as I pulled it away. "Are you working the Halloween Bash on Saturday?"

"No," Donnie said, the word so short that I looked up in surprise. There was a crease between his eyes. "I'm going with Phoebe from Calculus. I asked her the first week of October."

I closed my eyes quickly, because as soon as he'd said all that, I remembered him telling me. Worse, I remembered him *gushing* about it. About how he'd asked her, about how he'd been so nervous, and how she'd practically jumped up and down when she'd said yes. "I-I knew that."

But Donnie's voice soured. "You forgot I asked her? You helped me make a sign and everything, Blaire."

"I know, I know. It just—it slipped my mind."

In all honesty, I did have a lot going on lately. Especially that first week of October. The day Donnie asked Phoebe was the day after I received Dad's letter, mere hours before I broke up with Lucas. I hadn't even remembered that she said yes, or that he'd even asked.

I was the worst friend in the world.

I used my spoon to separate the clumpy guts from the side of the pumpkin, my fingers quickly going numb from the iciness of them. The seeds slipped between my fingers when I tried to pick them out, mushing with the rest of the innards. "Did you two say what you're going as?" I asked softly, trying to coax Donnie away from his anger.

His voice came out as a grumble as he hacked into his pumpkin. "We're going to be salt and pepper shakers."

I honestly wasn't surprised. "Are you going to be salt or pepper?"

"Did you know Hailey asked Lucas?"

I focused on keeping my face focused on my pumpkin. One of my shoulders, though, did raise on its own accord. "Asked him what?"

"Blaire. You know what."

Ugh. The dampness from the ground started to sink into the knees of my jeans, but I ignored it, gripping a ton of guts and slapping them in the bucket, not caring about the stupid seeds. "Fine, I did know, okay? Lucas told me at the corn maze." I tried, but I couldn't keep the heavy dose of sarcasm from lacing in my words. "And you know what? Good for them. They were a cute couple, weren't they? His dark hair practically matches her eyes. Perfect."

He still watched me closely. "She asked him. He didn't say yes."

No, but he said *he'd let her know.* Basically a maybe. Practically a yes. And after I'd told him to do it the other night, I'd be surprised if they hadn't gotten together and talked about it already. They probably already planned what they'd wear. Hey, maybe they'd reuse those mermaid costumes.

"I don't care, Donnie." I scooped everything out a little more angrily, the rind of the pumpkin vibrating with my movements. "I really don't. I mean, I was the one who dumped him. I did. I told him I didn't want to be with him anymore. Good for him if he goes out and finds someone else."

"Gosh, Blaire, would you stop that?"

I blinked up from my pumpkin, surprised by the sharpness in his voice.

Donnie put down his spoon and placed both hands on the pumpkin, eyes leveling to my own. "You haven't told me why you broke up with Lucas, which I can't figure out why you're keeping it from me, but that doesn't matter—what matters is that you're *lying.* You don't love Lucas anymore? Tell that to the look on your face every time you see him."

I didn't want to admit it, but I knew exactly what he meant. Every time I saw Lucas, it felt like I'd been punched. Left behind.

As Donnie went on, his voice rose in volume—or maybe that was me hearing the increasing severity in his tone. "You know, if you keep doing this, people are going to stop wanting to be around you. You can't hurt people and expect them to keep crawling back. This is your chance, Blaire. Tell me what's going on."

A dark emotion stirred in my chest, and I gripped the spoon so tightly that it could've been a weapon. Tell him the truth? He practically knew it anyway. Was it really hard to connect all those dots? "I'm sorry you're thrown in the middle of this," I said to him, voice laced with venom, and I didn't know where it'd come from. "But you're seeing what you want to see. Nothing's going on."

Donnie drew in a sharp breath, the curved line of his jaw flexing as he clenched it shut. He shoved to his feet. "You're on a fast track to pushing everyone away, you know. And then you're going to be alone, and whose fault would that be?"

Donnie stomped up onto his porch and threw open the screen door, leaving me kneeling on the ground by myself. My chest rose and fell rapidly, mostly out of shock than anything else. Donnie and I *never* fought. Not like that. Not that that constituted as a fight, but we hardly ever raised our voices with each other.

You're going to be alone, and whose fault would that be?

Eventually it would happen, but not yet, not now.

Except it *was* happening now. Lucas hadn't shown up today. Donnie had walked away from me. I was in the cold grass by myself, with nothing but the company of lumpy, orange pumpkins. I bit down on my lower lip, not hard enough to elicit true pain, but hard enough to keep the tears at bay.

Dad had never been any good at pushing people away,

so he'd left. I, on the other hand, seemed to be *too* good at pushing people away, but I could never bring myself to fully pull back from everyone. To be able to leave it all behind.

Being truly alone frightened me too much, but Donnie was right. I was on the fast track to being all by myself.

And instead of reversing off the path, I continued head-first.

ten

I ran my fingers over the flat of my nails, freshly painted its usual dark color and especially smooth, the simple fidget doing little to calm my nerves. Gram never liked it when I had my nails painted for parties —probably because the only color I owned was Midnight Black—but I always painted them in between. It made me feel more put-together, the cool polish on my nails so sooth- ing, grounding.

I went to first period Thursday morning with no espresso, for the first time in a long time. Donnie was punishing me, no doubt, wanting to show me what life would be like if I continued on my path of shoving people away. I didn't know how to tell him I couldn't help myself— everything had reached a boiling point and spilled over.

Donnie sat stonily beside me, the assigned seating chart forcing us to still be by each other. That didn't lessen his cold shoulder, though.

Mr. Miller was going on and on about Halloween,

talking about the pep rally tomorrow, about the Boo-Bash on Saturday, but I zoned out, tracing a sentence in Spanish with my pencil. Most of my classes were having a Halloween party in honor of the holiday, asking students to bring snacks or candy. I hadn't signed up for anything, even though Gram would just die to make Halloween-themed treats. I could see it now—she'd make a cookies-and-cream pudding, with crushed cookies on top looking like dirt and a zombie hand sticking out of it.

Maybe I should've asked her to make treats, but I didn't feel like carting around cookies and pudding and pretending Halloween was so fun. I didn't want to celebrate.

The costume theme today was Throwback Thursday— wear something from the decades. Donnie had gone with the 80s, wearing a brightly colored jogging suit he'd found at the thrift store, and he'd styled his curly black hair in a way that poofed on top.

He tried his hardest to appear focused on the work- sheet in front of him, but I watched as his pencil pretended to scribble, faint gray lines ghosting along paper. I reached over and wrote on the corner of his worksheet, writing in Spanish, *lo siento*.

I'm sorry.

He wasted no time scrubbing his eraser across where I'd written. Apology *not* accepted, apparently.

I sat back in my seat, listening to Mr. Miller go on about everything to do with the holiday that I couldn't wait to get over with. Donnie and I would go back to normal, the parties would start to die down, and Lucas and me...well, there would be no Lucas and me.

Everything would go back to the way it'd been before, except the letter, which still sat unopened at the bottom of my backpack.

You're going to be alone, and whose fault would that be?

Mine. Completely and totally mine.

Gram had shut herself in the costume room when I got home, and she'd been in there for a good part of the afternoon. She said she wanted to "spend some alone time with her fabric."

I clearly didn't get my sanity from her side of the family.

I sat on the living room couch with a notebook folded over in my lap, idly doodling as I listened to the TV. The hum of the voices oddly comforted me in the quietness of the apartment, especially because it filled my thoughts. I didn't focus on the fact that I had nothing to do. No homework to finish, no friends to text—nothing. So, instead of letting my thoughts get away from me, I doodled. Stupid things. Witch hats, trees with hanging apples, puffy little clouds. Just drew whatever came to me.

"Blaire?" Gram's voice came sudden, much louder than the voices on the TV, causing me to jump. "Can you run to Mrs. Avery's house and pick up our pitcher? She found it the other day—the one we were missing? She said she'd have it washed and ready. I'd go, but I'm working on the last alterations on a certain piece."

I glanced up from my notebook. "Do we need it now?"

"I need it for the Bash, and I want to get all our ducks in a row. Leaving things to the last minute makes me nervous—you know that." Her eyes fell to the notebook in my lap. "Working on anything fun?"

"Just goofing off."

Just keeping my mind off how everything sucks.

She hesitated, as if she hated that she was interrupting me. "You could grab the pitcher tomorrow if you wanted. I can see if Mrs. Avery can give it to Lucas—"

"It's totally fine, Gram," I said, flipping my notebook closed and pushing to my feet. "Her house isn't far. I'll be right back."

Hallow wasn't a big town, the Avery house only a few blocks from the apartment. The warmth from the previous few days had vanished, leaving the air a little frosty. The walk gave me ample time to admire the color-changing trees, the fall decorations. I traveled past a few kids raking leaves into a big pile, no doubt to jump in them later. I couldn't help but smile.

People had gone all out in terms of Halloween setups this year. Spiderwebs hung from trees, ghosts and witches strung up by pieces of string. Someone had even dug up a fake grave in their front yard—at least, I *hoped* it was a fake grave.

Mom and Dad used to go all out with decorations. Our entire house had been decked out with Halloween adornments, as well as leaves and other fall-themed things. Mom had had an obsession for those little scarecrow dolls and had liked to put them up everywhere. On the fireplace mantel, on the kitchen table—practically any flat surface in the house.

Dad used to always grumble and groan about them, saying they invaded his space, but I think he'd secretly liked them too. I'd never thought to ask.

I could still remember our last Halloween together. We'd spent the hour and a half passing out candy to little kids and then the rest of the night watching movies together. I'd told them it was the lamest thing ever—me being home on Halloween with my parents. I'd wanted to go to the Halloween Bash, hang out with Donnie, flirt with Lucas, but they'd loved the idea of us staying in together more.

I'd never admitted to them that I secretly loved it. Loved cuddling on the couch eating chocolate-covered popcorn, teasing about the quality of the movies. I'd never told either of them how much those moments had meant to me.

And now it was too late on both counts.

A thought whispered, *You could still tell your dad.*

I shoved the idea away, quickening my pace down the sidewalk.

The Averys had decorated their house tastefully for the holiday, with a few pumpkins lining the walkway up to their front porch. The pumpkins, instead of being carved, were painted with several shades of blue to spell out their last name.

My pulse jumped a little in my chest as I stepped up onto the porch, ringing for the doorbell.

Mrs. Avery pulled the wide oak door open, and something similar to disappointment bloomed inside me. "Blaire, good to see you," she greeted with a smile, pushing open the storm door. "I just got off the phone with your grandmother. Come inside, and I'll get the pitcher. Delia and I made hot cocoa. You have to have some before you go back."

I puffed on my cold fingers, stepping over the threshold. Heat wrapped around me in a comfortable, warm hug. "That would be amazing, Mrs. Avery. It's getting colder and colder out there."

Despite Lucas and I being broken up, it still felt extremely normal to walk into his front entryway like old times. I could almost pretend like nothing had changed.

But as soon as I stepped further into the house, a warm smell hit my nose, like cinnamon and spice and something a little nutty. The smell instantly triggered a memory, almost rendering me immobile over the threshold.

Again, the last Halloween we'd spent together as a family came to my mind, and the only reason the memory stood out in any sort of contrast was because I remembered Dad baking pumpkin seeds. Or, rather, *burning* pumpkin seeds, as the entire kitchen had had a hazy smoke over it. Dad had been completely unbothered, though, and had assured me that everything he did had a purpose.

"*I want them to smell like that,*" he'd told me, waving his hand to clear the air. "*Once you try them, you'll see.*"

And I remembered Mom, who sat at the kitchen table, merely smiled. "*Or you'll hate them, like me, but the smell— you can't hate the smell.*"

My chest now pinched so tight as I imagined Mom's cheery smile, the pitch of her voice. Remembered Dad's laugh, his confident pumpkin-seed baking.

"Mmm, those seeds are smelling so good." Mrs. Avery inhaled deeply as she headed toward the kitchen. She left me behind, my legs unwilling to follow. "Lucas and Delia love them. Speaking of, you can take a hot chocolate thermos home and give it back to Lucas tomorrow at school if you want."

I hadn't smelled the scent of baked pumpkin seeds in years. The sparking sensation of it almost made my world feel turned over, as if it toppled on its side and I'd lost my footing. I could imagine Mom, plain as day, smiling at me from the table. Dad leaning against the countertop, trying to convince the two of us that baked pumpkin seeds were the best thing in the world. "*Especially with cinnamon,*" I could practically hear him say in that deep tone of his.

And he'd smile like he'd told a joke, that wide and happy smile, completely contagious.

He'd flip my hair over my shoulder and say, "*Once you try them, you'll see, Blaire.*"

Everything in me shuddered as a fissure worked its way through my chest, cracking a jagged line from my stomach to my throat.

"Mom, who are you talking—Blaire? What are you doing here?"

I looked up to find Lucas on the other end of the hallway, poking his head out from his bedroom door. His dark hair was ruffled, as if he'd just gotten done running his fingers through it. I could almost imagine him tugging at their ends.

Lucas could look at me and *know.* As he came closer, eyes tracing whatever expression rested on my face—I was too numb to be able to feel it—the line between his brows thickened. "What's wrong?"

So many things, I wanted to say. *Donnie and I are fighting, and we never fight. And I miss you—I miss you so much that it hurts to breathe. I got a letter from my dad, and I'm too afraid to open it—too afraid it's going to make me forgive him.*

I kept my mouth shut, not letting the words escape.

"Here's the pitcher for your grandmother, and the thermos for you," Mrs. Avery said as she came back out into the hallway, offering me both items. She spotted Lucas. "Oh, I pulled your pumpkin seeds from the oven. They looked done."

His blue eyes flicked over to her. "Thanks, Mom."

Mrs. Avery's attention went back to me—or, namely, back to the items she still held out to me. The thermos and the pitcher. I hadn't taken them. "Blaire?"

In that moment, I felt like a ghost, a shadowy figure spotted from the corner of someone's eye, easily dismissible due to an overactive imagination. There, but not there.

Seen, but not seen. Because Lucas and his mother saw me clearly, standing directly in front of them, but they didn't see *me*. Breaking apart, dissolving to the thoughts that rummaged in my brain, lost in the wave of negativity. Drowning.

I took the thermos and the pitcher, my fingers shaking as they curled over each item. Though my hands quivered, my voice did not. It sounded stiff and formal, but not shaky. "Thank you, Mrs. Avery. I'll make sure to give the thermos to Lucas tomorrow." My boots squeaked on the wood floor as I stepped backward. I slipped the thermos into the crook of my elbow to open the door. "Have a good night."

As I stepped out into the October air, I sucked in a shallow breath, the action felt dooming, absolute. And I couldn't figure out why. Why would shutting the door on Lucas's house feel like a final goodbye?

It didn't take long to figure out why. Because for the first time when I walked away, Lucas didn't follow.

I stared at the ceiling fan that hung from the middle of my room, counting the lazy rotations it made. Shadows cast strange images on the walls, and sometimes when the occasional car would pass, their headlights would glance off my window. My eyes drooped, but I couldn't quite close them all the way. Couldn't quite turn my brain off.

My body had been still for a while now, long enough for there to be an ache blooming in my hip. I knew I needed to go to sleep—I had school in the morning—but I was a light bulb with a broken switch. I was a bottle of soda, shaken up, ready to explode.

I could've screamed—screamed a rasping noise that scraped my throat raw. The pressure of it built in my chest. It rested there, on the tip of my tongue, and yet...it never came out.

I watched the fan spin once, twice, around and around.

Why was everything falling apart? Why couldn't some semblance of my old life remain? When things had been easy, good, happy. No trace of those things existed now. Donnie, Lucas, Dad. All the boys in my life.

What would your perfect life look like? my brain whispered, its soothing voice almost hypnotic as the ceiling fan spinning. *Donnie, Lucas, Dad—how would those pieces fit into your life differently than right now?*

Well, for one thing, Donnie would be on my side of things. I took his never-budging loyalty for granted. Or, apparently, his loyalty *was* budging. Either way, I'd have him in my life. I'd have him not be mad at me. I'd win his forgiveness, and we'd go back to normal.

Lucas. My perfect life with Lucas...what would that look like? I could imagine him pulling up in front of the apartment, Crushed Beanz coffees already in the cup holders, the scent filling the car. His hand warm in mine, squeezing my fingers playfully as he walked me to class. His skin against mine, lips offering a glancing kiss.

And as for Dad, he *definitely* wouldn't be sending me letters. He'd left, and he thought he could send a letter and everything was better? Not cool.

Though, maybe my perfect life with him had him *in* it. Present. Back home, waking me up on Saturday mornings with a plate of breakfast set at the table. Warm eyes. Teasing grin.

But perfect lives didn't exist. Entertaining the idea was self-torture.

My gaze drifted from the ceiling fan to fall to the corner of my bedroom, to the exact place where my back-pack sat half-zipped. The skulls printed on the fabric basi-cally screamed *keep away*, but I couldn't get the elephant in the room to disappear.

It was after midnight—October 30th. Two years ago to the day, Dad had finalized everything. Called Gram and asked if we could stay the night. Started packing. Started planning his life without me. And on October 31st, it'd offi-cially be two years ago that he'd left.

Gram had told me to read the letter. Lucas had told me to read the letter. If Donnie knew about it, I was sure he'd be saying something as well.

Mom would've told me to read it too, but in a much different way. *Don't read it for him,* she'd say in that tone of voice that always put my raging insides in a time-out. *Read it for you. You're driving yourself crazy wondering. The stress of it is changing you, honey. Just read it so you can sleep.*

The blades on the fan spun, an endless cycle.

Just read it so I could sleep.

I slipped the covers back as silently as I could and exposed my legs to the cool air. The heater must've kicked off. I didn't bother pushing my toes into my slippers before walking to my backpack. The room was filled with a blue sort of darkness, but I had no trouble finding the orange envelope underneath my textbooks. I drew it out, blood humming, and made my way back to my bed.

Just so I can sleep, I told myself as I lifted the envelope, tracing the handwriting with my index finger. *B L A I R E.* All capitals.

I didn't have to respond; I didn't have to forgive him. I wasn't reading it for him, for Gram, for Lucas, or for Donnie. I was reading it for me.

With a hard jerk, I slid my finger along the seal, tearing it open.

eleven

Dear Blaire,

    I've never written a letter before, so I hope you can forgive how messy it is. I wrote you a note once, on the back of a gas station receipt. "Blaire, you know I love you. I can't be in Hallow anymore. I'm sorry." I think about how you must've woken up on the morning of Halloween, expecting me to be there, but I was gone.

    I wish I could say I know what you think, but I don't. I can't read your mind anymore; I can't even imagine what you must be thinking and feeling, seeing this letter. But I didn't leave because I didn't love you. I hope and pray to God you never thought that. Your mother was the love of my life, you know. Losing her was...hard, for both of us. I wish I'd spoken to you more after she passed, Blaire. Maybe things would've been different if I had spoken to someone—to you.

I MADE SOME BAD DECISIONS AFTER SHE DIED. I WASN'T IN MY RIGHT MIND. GRAM WILL ATTEST TO THAT IF YOU ASK—IF SHE HASN'T ALREADY TOLD YOU. I KNEW IT WASN'T IN YOUR BEST INTEREST TO BE AROUND ME. AND I KNOW WHAT YOU'RE THINKING. THAT SOUNDS LIKE COMPLETE BULL CRAP. I KNOW. BUT IF IT CAME DOWN TO WHO YOU WERE BETTER OFF WITH, IT WOULDN'T HAVE BEEN WITH ME.

YOU'RE PROBABLY WONDERING WHY I'M REACHING OUT NOW, BUT I'VE BEEN SOBER NINETY DAYS. I TOLD MYSELF I COULDN'T REACH OUT UNTIL THEN. I KNOW IT'S NOT FAIR OF ME TO SAY, BUT I WILL BE THERE IF YOU NEED ANYTHING, BLAIRE. WHATEVER YOU NEED. IF YOU WANT ME TO COME HOME, I'LL COME, IN A HEARTBEAT. IF YOU WANT TO NEVER SEE ME AGAIN, I'LL STAY AWAY. JUST NO MATTER WHAT, KNOW THAT I LOVE YOU. AND I'M SORRY. FOR EVERYTHING.

DAD

* * *

I didn't leave my room.

The clock read seven-thirty when Gram knocked on my door Friday morning, probably wondering why I hadn't emerged yet. I'd still been curled up on my bed, pressing Dad's letter to my chest. I'd been like that for a while—long enough to hear the birds begin to chirp, to see the sun peek through my curtains. She knocked twice, but I couldn't lift my voice high enough to answer. I waited for her to poke her head in, to ask me if I was getting around for school, but she never did.

Everything sounded muffled, muted, numb. I tried to take stock of how I felt, but my thoughts were fluid, water slipping through my fingers, fog dissipating in a morning breeze.

Everything was quiet; everything was still.

My bedroom was nothing fancy. After two years to the day of living with Gram, I'd never gotten around to fully decorating it. My old bedroom had been much bigger than this one, so I'd ended up having to donate most of the furniture when the house had gone up for sale. I'd always struggled with the idea of making this bedroom feel homey, like *mine*, but now as I stared at my surroundings, I wished there was something in it that brought me comfort.

I didn't have any pictures of my parents hung up, no pictures of Lucas or Donnie, no posters. Clothes littered the ground, my hamper overflowed in the corner, but nothing screamed *me*. For two years, I'd lived in this room and hadn't done a single thing to make it mine. Hadn't painted the walls, hadn't even bought a rug.

It wasn't like I'd ever be able to move back home. The house had sold within the first year.

I felt disconnected from the world lying on my bed, listening to the dull thumping of my heartbeat in my ears. A fire lit behind my eyes, a silent cue tears would should be flowing, but I hadn't cried yet. For some reason, I couldn't. I'd been pushing it all down for so long that I'd almost forgotten how to cry.

What was Dad doing right now? Waiting for the postal service to drop off the mail, hoping he'd receive a letter from me? Sitting by the phone, hoping it'd ring? Eating cereal? Going to his day job? Did he even *have* a day job?

That man seemed almost like a stranger now. He'd written that he was ninety days sober, but the Dad I remembered had never struggled with addiction. Not that I'd known. Was it something triggered by losing Mom? Was it alcohol or something else? Could that be why he'd left in the first place?

I had so many questions, and none would get answers. Not unless I wrote a letter back.

My cord was totally unplugged from the outlet, disconnected from the energy that'd fueled me.

My bedroom door creaked open, and I'd been lost in my thoughts for who knew how long. It'd been a while since Gram last checked on me; she must've decided she needed to make sure I was visibly okay.

Footsteps came further into the room, loud on the creaky floors, until my bed dipped as Gram sat down. I had my back to her, the orange envelope tucked out of sight.

"This day sucks," a voice said, a voice that was *not* Gram's, and I jerked to look over my shoulder. Donnie sat on the edge of my bed, his dark hair spiked up every which way, exactly how he liked it.

And...I had no idea what he was wearing.

He was in one of those black, full-body suits, but also had strapped a pair of wings to his back. Not butterfly wings or fairy wings, though—no, they were *moth* wings. They looked kind of like butterfly wings little kids normally wore, but painted dark colors. He had a faux fur scarf around his neck, one he'd totally stolen from our costume trunk. On his head, he wore a crown of pipe-cleaner antennas, bent at strange angles.

"I know," Donnie said seriously, expression unflinching. "You're amazed at my costume."

I didn't even know what to say. "What are you doing here? Aren't you supposed to be at school?"

"Well." Donnie pulled up one leg, resting it on my bed, and angling his body toward mine. "Gram called Aimee, who came and signed me out of first period. Which kind of sucks, because today was our Halloween party, and I was definitely going to win best costume."

Despite everything, I found myself wanting to smile, though it never made it to the surface. "Why would she sign you out?"

He raised an eyebrow. "Why do you think?"

My stomach tightened, discomfort making me shift. "I'm not allowed one mental health day without everyone freaking out?" I asked, voice crossing over into the realm of irritation. "You didn't have to leave school because I didn't get out of bed this morning."

"You know, it makes sense now."

"*What* makes sense?"

"Why you've been in a terrible mood." Donnie's gaze slipped away from my face to rest by my side. "Aimee told me about *that*."

The orange envelope had completely slipped into view, demanding attention. I scrambled for it, trying to press it behind my covers. It didn't matter; Donnie had already seen. "Aunt Aimee knows about it?"

"I'm assuming Gram told her," he said, leaning his palm onto my bed. "But what I don't get is why *you* didn't tell *me*."

I pushed up to lean against my headboard, pulling my legs to my chest. Donnie deserved a better answer, but I didn't have one. "I don't know."

"Okay, why didn't you tell Lucas?"

"I don't know," I said again, my irritation morphing into a sterner sort of frustration.

But Donnie wasn't done pushing. "Why did you break up with Lucas?"

I let out a sharp sigh. "Because we almost went all the way."

If I could've taken a picture of that exact moment, I would've. Donnie jolted, his wings flapping with the movement, eyes circling wide. He seemed to be frozen, lips parted as if at any moment he'd begin to speak, but he didn't. At least, not for several moments.

And then— "I'm sorry, *what*?"

I cringed, wrapping my arms around my legs. "Do I have to say it again?"

"I mean—I don't—" Donnie stopped, closed his mouth. Took in a breath. Tried again. "When?"

"The night before I broke things off."

"Why would that make you want to break up with him?" His voice changed in an instant, from confused to angry. "Did he pressure you—"

"No!" Now I buried my face into the space between my knees and my chest, the shadows there eclipsing the flush that swallowed my face. My toes curled against my blankets, already cringing. "I...I was the one to—you know. Go for it."

I could practically hear Donnie's frown. "So...he rejected you? That's why you broke up with him?"

It was easier to talk to him with my face covered, easier to pretend like I wasn't talking to him about *this*. "No, he didn't reject me. Gram called me and we stopped."

Donnie snorted a little. "You got blocked by your grandma."

My shoulders slumped as I looked up at him through the barest of slivers between my forehead and my arm.

Donnie sat back a little, the momentary amusement on his face filtering into a sober expression. "So if he didn't reject you, why did you two break up?"

"You know, I'd done a fantastic job at not being sad," I said, fully lifting my head, nudging my hair from my eyes. My focus fell on a crack in the plaster wall on the other side of me, and I didn't look away. "After everything had happened, I was fine. I mean, it sucked—the stuff with Mom and Dad. I was just starting to get used to my new life and enjoy where I was at when Dad's letter came in the mail. And everything just...fell apart."

Donnie traced his fingertips on the blanket near the side of my foot, not close enough to tickle but close enough to feel it. "How so?"

The feeling I'd gotten when I'd seen the envelope for

the first time swept back into my system, and a soreness crept into my throat, making it nearly impossible to swallow. "It reminded me you can love someone with all your heart, and they can still leave you."

My mind drifted back to that day, when realization had doused me like a bucket of ice water. I'd pulled the letter out of the mail slot without thinking twice, carrying it all the way up into the apartment before actually looking at it. And when I had, the air in my lungs had thickened, like I'd breathed through sludge.

"I loved Dad with all of my heart, and he could still just walk away. And I realized Lucas could, too." The words had dropped off to a whisper, my eyes burning from staring at one spot for so long. The soreness in my throat intensified, each breath I took in nearly choking.

"That's why you've been pushing him away," Donnie grasped. "You were pushing him away so he couldn't leave you first."

Hearing him say it aloud sounded *awful*. Selfish. Cruel. Stupid. I wanted to jump to deny it, because no way all of my feelings and motives boiled down to that single idea, but no words came out.

That night when I'd left Lucas's house, my body still riding the high of what almost was, I'd been on top of the world. Saying those three words in high school felt ridiculous to me, but I *did* love Lucas. I could see a future with him. Sure, the future had been cloudy with uncertainty, but I'd been able to see one.

Receiving Dad's letter had introduced a new fear,

though. What if I wasn't enough for Lucas too? What if, after everything, he ended up walking away? Throwing in the towel? Leaving me like Dad?

The mere idea had made me so panicked.

"That's a load of crap, you know that?"

I looked at Donnie sharply. "What?"

"Blaire, I know you wear the costume a lot, but you're no princess. You're a butt-kicking girl who holds her own. Crap happens to you, but you're strong." Donnie shrugged a little, and his wing bobbled. "Yeah, Lucas breaking up with you would suck. And I'd be thrown into the middle again, which would suck almost as bad because all of this has been totally awkward, but you'd get through it. You'd be okay."

His words were kind, and he sounded so sure, but I wasn't convinced. My words came out small. "How do you know?"

"Because you have me," Donnie said with a smile. "And Gram. And you've gone through crap over the past two years—*on top of* going through high school, which is miserable. You're strong. Your life doesn't revolve around a guy, and you know that."

I wanted to repel everything he said, wanted to shake the thoughts out of my head. Wanted to wallow in this moment of pain and suffering, because I deserved it. For hurting Lucas so badly, I deserved it. For not opening Dad's letter sooner, I deserved it. Thinking about Lucas deciding to walk away had opened a rift in my chest, almost uncrossable. Too wide of a distance to function.

Before he let me stew even further in my thoughts, Donnie said, "Besides, I don't think you have to worry about him walking away, Blaire. I mean, he stuck around even when you dumped him, didn't he? He still got you Crushed Beanz every morning."

Back up the truck. Lucas had done— "*What?*"

"You mean you really thought *I* got you coffee every morning?" He winked. "Blaire, I love you, but not enough to wake up fifteen minutes earlier. You think beauty like this just *happens?*"

His words weren't computing. Complete gibberish. "So this entire time, Lucas has still been getting me coffee?"

"Except for that one day—the one where the coffee was super sweet? I got it that time. He was running late and paid me fifteen bucks."

So Donnie was saying that even though we'd been broken up, Lucas had still gotten us coffee every morning? Me *and* Donnie? My usual drink. Lucas had gotten it right every time. I recalled the days when Lucas had had a cup of his own in his hand, the teal Crushed Beanz logo a dead giveaway.

My stomach fluttered, butterflies tumbling around. I glanced away, not trusting myself to look at Donnie—not trusting that my gaze wasn't filled with some sort of sappy emotion—and focused on the orange envelope by my side. I had it turned so Dad's handwriting faced me, stark black letters.

"Dad wrote a nice letter," I told Donnie, changing the subject and not looking up. The frown I held on my face began to quiver as emotion pushed through me, the line in my forehead trembling with the effort to keep severe. "Said that if I wanted to reach out, I could. I used to be so angry at him for sending it—for ruining everything, but...I'm not angry anymore."

No, that anger had disappeared, burnt up. The black smoke of my resentment had faded, leaving different emotions in its wake. Not as choking as the smoke; hazy like fog on a fall morning. There was a promise that it would clear, and if I looked hard enough, I could somewhat see down the road.

But in the wake of anger rested *pain*.

I tried not to let myself cry too much. Crying felt so useless, pointless, childish. I wasn't much of a crier, anyway —when something bad happened, I didn't get sad. I pushed everything down, shoved it away, refused to deal with it.

But now that pain swamped through me, threatening to drown me. All the pain came out through my tears. The coolness tracked its way down my hot cheeks, and a teardrop fell onto my blankets. It was the silent sort of cry. *Mourning*. All the grief from Mom, all the grief from Dad, all the grief from Lucas, culminating into a slicing ache.

Donnie reached out and wrapped his hand over the curve of my knee, giving it a squeeze, hanging on.

In a way, crying everything out was refreshing. A thunderstorm after a long season of drought. The gasping breaths I took felt like the first in a long time—the first, perhaps, since Dad had left. At least the first since I'd received his letter.

Dad had realized he couldn't face Halloween in Hallow without her. And I saw that now. It was what he'd written on a gas station receipt from that same day, but I'd never understood. *Blaire, you know I love you. I can't be in Hallow anymore. I'm sorry.* He couldn't stay in Hallow because it reminded him too much of Mom. Of everything she'd loved, every place she'd been, the very house she'd lived in. It hadn't been about me. And no matter how much I wanted to—and I really did—I couldn't fault him for his fear. He'd left town because he'd been afraid to face the holiday without Mom.

I'd broken up with Lucas because I was afraid of the pain of him walking away, a pain that might've not ever happened.

Fear made people do crazy, stupid things.

For the first time in two years, I stared through Dad's eyes with startling clarity. Part of me wanted to pretend otherwise, the begrudging, bitter part, but I knew the truth. For what felt like the first time, my heart ached *for* Dad.

"Is everything—Blaire?" Gram's voice was quiet at first, and then morphed into a more concentrated level of concern. "Sweetheart, what's wrong?"

Donnie stood from the bed to let Gram sit down, and she pulled me into her arms. After a moment of stiffness, unused to her embrace, my body relaxed. Her vanilla perfume washed over me immediately, her house robe gentle against my cheek.

Without another word, Donnie slipped from the room.

It'd been a long time since Gram had held me like this,

like an upset child, and I found myself clinging to her. I couldn't remember the last time I'd melted into her. There was something about a grandmother's hug that was *perfect*. Her hugs reminded me of Mom's, where a simple embrace made the whole world seem better, brighter. The world started spinning regularly again; the air in my lungs cleared.

A part of me, the part so used to pushing people away, wanted to hide the envelope, tuck it behind my back, not let Gram know I'd read it. That part of me didn't want her to be right, didn't want her to know I'd caved.

I drew in a breath that rattled. "I read Dad's letter."

Immediately, her grip on me tensed. "You don't have to answer him, you know. Not until you're ready to. There isn't a time limit or an expiration date or anything like that."

I pulled away enough so I could see her face, swiping my palm along my cheeks. It came away damp. "I don't know if I'll write back. Not yet. I think...I think I still need to wrap my head around it."

She pushed my hair over my shoulder, then grasped the tops of my arms, giving them an affectionate squeeze. "You're growing into such a fine young woman, you know that? Your parents...they'd be proud."

Great, I was going to start crying again. "Did you know Dad was struggling?" I asked her, thinking about his letter. "Before he left, I mean."

"I knew he was having a hard time, but I never dreamed he'd leave us." Gram still smoothed her fingers through my hair, the lulling movement comforting. "If I'd known, I would've talked him out of it."

I tried to think what I might've done differently if I'd known Dad was going to leave that night. What if I'd come out into the kitchen and saw him writing that note? What would I have done? Would that have changed anything? I would never know.

Gram cleared her throat, and her eyes were bright. "I've got a surprise for you. I wanted to save it until tomorrow, but I think you need something to make you smile today."

I swiped the back of my hand across my cheek. "What is it?"

"I've kept the surprise quite well," she said smugly, her hands sliding down to grab mine. "But I think you need to try it on to see it in the full effect."

"Try it on?" I frowned a little, sniffling. "Is it for Costume Catering?"

Gram smiled. "Come on, I'll show you. First, can I ask you a question?" She lowered her voice. "What was Donnie wearing?"

A laugh burst out of me, strangled but genuine. "It was costume week at school. He was a moth, I think."

"Costume week! Why didn't you say anything? I'm the queen of costumes! We could've come up with fun ideas."

"Next year," I promised her, knowing it wasn't a hollow Halloween promise. I allowed her to draw me to my feet. "Now, about that surprise?"

twelve

That night, despite not sleeping at all the night before, I couldn't fall asleep. Tonight, though, I wasn't tormented by the idea of opening Dad's letter.

No, I was instead tormented by Lucas.

More like the idea of Lucas. I'd seen him yesterday when I'd picked up the pitcher for Gram, but it already felt like a lifetime ago.

Even though I wanted to call him, I wasn't sure I could. I understood what Donnie had said earlier—my life didn't revolve around a guy. If Lucas wanted to leave, it wouldn't ruin my life. Even still, the fear was still there. That nagging idea of "what if?" What if I let him back in only to get hurt again? What if we broke up a month later? What if he didn't want me back?

With the Halloween Bash tomorrow, I had no idea if Lucas had accepted Hailey's proposal to be her date. After everything I'd put him through—after I'd told him he *should*—he deserved someone who wanted his company. In all honesty, I couldn't remember why they'd ever broken up in the first place. And if I couldn't remember why, it must not have been a big enough deal. Maybe it was a hurdle they could easily overcome; maybe they already had.

When I thought I couldn't take it anymore and that my brain was about to explode, I rolled over, pushing onto one elbow and reaching toward my nightstand. My cell phone laid right on top of the envelope, Dad's letter tucked safely inside. I still didn't know if I wanted to write him back or not, but I couldn't help but feel protective of the letter now. Protective of the words he'd written for me.

Funny how I'd wanted to throw the thing away.

I swiped up my cell, and as I unlocked the screen, it started vibrating. My heart nearly jumped out of my chest as I saw Lucas's name flash, along with the picture I'd set to his contact info. It'd originally been a photo of us after one of his football games last year, posing under the stadium lights, but I'd cropped it, so it only showed him.

I got so distracted by the photo that the call almost went to voicemail before I pressed accept. For a moment, I watched my phone, slowly lifting it to my ear as if it were about to explode. "Hello?"

"It's after midnight." Lucas's voice came immediately, without hesitation. "Happy Halloween."

A quick glance at my alarm clock told me he wasn't wrong. "Happy Halloween." My heart beat so loudly in my ears that I almost couldn't hear myself speak. "Did you wait up so you could call me at midnight?"

"I might've been."

A pause filled the air, and I hated it. Our lingering history clung to the quiet, filling the moment with white noise. "You know, we never went on our fourth outing," I told him, running my fingertips through my hair.

"After the corn maze, I wasn't sure—well, I wasn't sure if we should've been friends anymore."

There it was. Lucas finally admitting what I knew early on—being friends wouldn't have worked. Was he admitting what I always feared? That he was finally done being a part of my life?

"Listen, I...I wanted to call and say I'm going to the Halloween Bash tomorrow."

My stomach flipped. "Me too. I have to work it."

"Oh. Really? They booked Gram for it this year?"

This time, when he claimed Gram as his own, I didn't correct him. "Yeah." I wanted to tell him about her excitement, how she'd practically screamed when she'd gotten the email, but the words choked off.

"She's probably so excited. That's so awesome." Lucas cleared his throat, speaking a bit firmer. "I'm going to wear that god-awful Prince Charming costume Mom got me. I—I forgot to get a different outfit. It's either that or the mermaid tail."

I pressed my fingers to my lips, trying to think of something to say. "Tight pants and everything?"

Lucas's laugh came through the other line, genuine, and it cracked apart the tenseness in me. For a split second, things felt normal. If only for a second. "Tight pants is better than no pants."

"I can't wait to see it," I said with a small smile, but it quickly faded. He'd wear that prince costume tomorrow—did that mean Hailey was going to be a princess? Were they going together? But why would he tell me he was going to be a prince? "Lucas, I—"

"I know how hard today is for you," he said abruptly, and I wished so, so badly that I could see his face, see what expression he had on, what emotion glimmered in his eyes. The phone provided a cruel barrier between us, shutting me out of what went on in that head of his. And gosh, I wanted to know what ran through his brain. "I just wanted to make sure you were okay."

The breath I drew in pinched, but it wasn't painful. "I'll be okay," I said softly, tucking my blanket closer to my skin. "Thanks, Lucas."

"I'll see you tomorrow, then," he said softly, a thread of hesitation tied in those words. I didn't want him to hang up, didn't want this strange phone call to end. "Goodnight, Blaire."

And without waiting for my response, Lucas ended the call.

I laid back against my pillows, staring at the ceiling much like I had last night. If I focused, his low voice still echoed in my ear. Why had he called me? To tell me he was going to be a prince at the Bash? To simply wish me Happy Halloween? After our argument at the corn maze, I couldn't imagine him doing the latter.

Had he told me he was being a prince because he

wanted me to be a princess? Was *that* it? Or was I over-thinking that too?

I thought of the surprise Gram had been crafting for me. I couldn't be a princess tomorrow, not even if I wanted to. For the first time in my life, I was going to be the one thing I'd always dreamed of.

The Village of Hallow went all out with the Halloween Boo-Bash each year. Our apartment was directly across the street from the park, making it hard to miss the big party. The music came through the brick walls, the laughter too, beckoning me to come to the window and take a peek. And so I'd go to the window, part the curtains, look out at the party in the park below. It always looked so strange, with so many people wandering around, fully in costume, laughing and having a great time.

However, being *at* the party was so much different than *watching* the party.

Or, at least, that's what I thought as I looked out the shop's windows, listening to Gram count off the last mini caramel cheesecakes. I rubbed my fingertips along the surface of my nail polish, lost in thought as I stared across the street. "There were a lot of trick-or-treaters this year," I said to Gram, watching the orange and black balloons wiggle with the wind. "I can't believe we ran out of candy so early."

"Well, they'll go across the street to the Boo-Bash and get their fill," she said with a chuckle, picking up a large pan of mini cheesecakes. "Aimee!" she shouted, turning to face the direction of the kitchen. "We're heading over!"

Aunt Aimee moved out from behind the wall that obscured the back, a jack-o-lantern apron covering her costume. She dressed as some kind of superhero, with a black-and-gray suit and a red cape that hung off her shoulders. "I'll head over with the last tray in a bit. John should be there manning the display."

Gram drew in a breath, nodding several times. "Great, great. Don't forget to grab the extra—"

"—skewers for the finger-foods," Aunt Aimee finished for her, rolling her eyes. "Go, Mom. Stop stressing."

"Yeah, it's going to be great," I told Gram with a smile. "Take a breath."

"Take a breath," Gram echoed, huffing a little, but did breathe in through her nose. "Can you grab the door?"

"Wait!" Aunt Aimee ducked back behind the wall, and when she emerged, she was holding a thin-bristled black broom. It was the one that we usually swept the kitchen with. "Since you don't have a hat to make it obvious, you need to have this."

I ducked to hide my wide smile as she passed it to me, my heart full. "Thanks, Aunt Aimee."

The costume I wore was so much more comfortable than the normal princess getup Gram liked to shove me in, and when I'd put it on and looked at myself in the mirror, my heart could've burst.

Gram stopped, about to pass through the doorway,

turning to look me in the eye. "I should've let you be a witch sooner, huh?"

Gram had outdone herself. I'd dressed in a shadow, a garment of darkness so much like me that I couldn't wipe a smile off my face as soon as I'd put it on. The black dress hung down to my feet, pooling there, making it look as if I were rising from the ground. Small shoulder pads had been sewn under the long sleeves, lace-covered to make it look spookier. The lace accent was also on the hem of the sleeves, and it tickled my skin. The layers of the dress slipped gently against my legs as I walked, the smooth fabric like silk.

All in all, I loved it.

"Come on," Gram said, stepping out further into the Halloween air, the costume she'd worn to Mrs. Avery's tea party flowing with her. "Let's go give them *pumpkin* to talk about."

My smile stretched to a full-blown grin, and I shook my head. "*Punny.*"

I'd predicted that Halloween would be a chilly one this year, but Mother Nature had gifted the Village of Hallow a beautifully tempered atmosphere, chilly enough to be seasonally *right*. Enough of a breeze to rustle the leaves along the ground, adding to the air of the spooky night.

I trailed behind Gram hesitantly, almost wanting to hide behind her as we approached the park. Despite my positive attitude over my outfit, nerves tried to devour me. Would I stumble upon Lucas—or, more specifically, Lucas and Hailey? I tried to tell myself that whatever happened, everything would be okay. If he was with her, that would be okay. And if he was alone...it'd be okay.

It didn't feel okay. More like nerve-wracking and world-ending.

Gram looked both ways before we crossed the street, giving us a good view of how many people were crammed into the park's boundaries. Monsters and vampires and witches and doctors—all the costumes under the sun—flitted around the space, mingling, having fun. The Halloween Boo-Bash was open to all ages, going from seven-thirty when trick-or-treating ended until ten at night. It was almost eight now, and the celebration of Halloween was in full swing. I even saw Delia running around with a few other kids from town, wearing the princess dress Gram and I had given her. She hadn't noticed me, laughing as she chased a boy in a homemade frog costume, with green jeans and a green sweatshirt, trying to reach out and grab his shoulder.

With a secret smile, I continued to trail Gram.

Whoever had decorated the park deserved an award. Someone had scattered pumpkins and jack-o-lanterns tastefully around the benches and picnic tables, and thick wads of fake spiderwebs hung from the tips of tree branches. Purple-and-orange neon lights rounded the perimeter of the stone fountain, glowing onto the sidewalk.

We found Uncle John in the section of the park that had been cordoned off for food, and I grinned when I saw his simple costume. He wore chef's whites complete with an authentic-looking toque blanche on his head, and I had no idea where he'd gotten it.

Donnie looked so much like his dad—they both had the same crazy hair, same goofy grin. When Uncle John spotted us, he lifted his palms. "Whatcha think, ladies? Pretty cool, huh?"

"Very on brand," Gram agreed as she came closer, chuckling. "Though, you don't match Aimee very well."

"I thought she could dress up as a mouse, but she vetoed that idea real quick." Uncle John winked at me. "Who knew Gram had a gothic princess costume?" he teased.

I put my hands on my hips. "I'm a *witch*."

"If the broom fits," a familiar voice said from behind me, and Donnie stepped up, grinning.

The costume he wore exceeded my expectations. Donnie ended up being the salt to Phoebe's pepper, because he had on a white cone-shaped costume, completed with a silver hat that acted as the dispenser on his head.

With Donnie by my side, I could almost pretend the nerves disappeared. Almost. "Where's your date?"

"Bathroom. I saw you and Gram and wanted to come say hi. Did you know they're letting adults into the bouncy house?" He rubbed his palms together, excitement dancing across his face. "It's going to be amazing."

Gram took stock of everything on our table, from the zombie cookies to the mini hot-dogs wrapped in bacon. "I'm going to see if Aimee needs any more help hauling the rest over." When she turned to face me, though, something caught her attention. Something behind me, over my shoulder. "Blaire."

I instantly knew.

I let out a shaking breath as I slowly pivoted on my heel, facing the party of people. From where I stood, everything was in plain sight. The black-and-orange balloon arch that hung above one of the park entrances—the idea totally stolen from Mrs. Avery's tea party, I was sure—the ample amount of Halloween decorations scattered around, and even the glowing orange cloths that covered a few waist-high tables. I could see everything.

Especially the boy who stood probably fifteen feet from me, dressed like royalty, stiff as a statue.

Lucas couldn't have been any more wrong about the costume his mom had laid out for him. "*Lame,*" he'd said. "*Tight pants.*" But it wasn't lame at all, and his pants weren't too tight. They were crimson red, with little gold stripes running down the leg. He wore a royal blue overcoat with tassels and shoulder pads. A red sash ran diagonally across his chest, secured at his waist. On his dark head of hair rested a golden crown.

He definitely looked like a prince, so much so that it took my breath away. My heart spurred faster in my chest with the step I took toward him, leaving Gram, Donnie, and Uncle John behind without a second thought. A frantic beat pounded against my ribs, leaving the world uneven, like everything had started listing to the side.

When I got to the edge of the cobblestones, mere feet

from Lucas, I stopped. The clocktower bell tolling above us as it reached the hour.

"You got your Halloween wish, I see." Lucas smiled, teeth and all. "No princess costumes for you."

Energy jolted through my body, humming, unable to keep fully still. I rubbed my fingers over my nails, the smoothness calming me, if only fractionally. "I owe you an apology," I said to him. "I need to apologize about what happened—about our breakup."

Lucas dragged in a shaking breath, and then he held his hand out. "Come with me."

Five fingers spread wide, angled toward me. Beckoning me. I knew what it'd mean if I took his hand, if I allowed myself to dive back in. Despite everything, I wasn't sure. "Where's Hailey?"

"Hailey?" Lucas blinked, a crease between his forehead. "I'm not here with her, Blaire. I—I'm here by myself."

"You are?"

"I told her I couldn't go with her." Lucas's face was somber, as serious as it had been the day I'd told him I couldn't be with him anymore. "She wasn't the one I wanted to be with."

For a split second, I was thrown back to that day, to that moment. That exact moment when the words had tumbled from my mouth, and I'd watched his face go from concerned to alarmed, worried to panicked at the idea of me breaking up with him. He'd reached out for me, as if a mere touch would wipe my words out of existence.

In that moment, I'd pulled back, afraid his touch would do that very thing.

I slid my hand into his, the warmth of his grasp flooding over me, starting from my hand and working its way up through my entire body. Without wasting a second, I entwined my fingers with his, holding on.

I tried to angle my face down, focusing on the way Lucas's hand curved over mine as he led me away from the crowd's center. His skin was darker than mine, my fingers were slenderer than his, but our hands fit together perfectly. Like a song I hadn't heard in years, but I still knew all the words to. A scent I hadn't smelled in forever, bringing back a flood of memories. Two puzzle pieces, molded together in a perfect fit.

People ambled by us as if we were ghosts passing in the night, but I didn't lift my gaze to see if anyone looked at us. Most wouldn't have thought anything of a couple wandering around.

I jolted. *A couple.*

Lucas pulled us around the edge of the clocktower, into a darker corner beneath one of the weeping willow trees. Its branches nearly touched the ground, overgrown and swaying in the breeze. Lucas, despite my death grip, released my fingers, facing me while straightening his shoulders. "I—"

"Let me go first," I said, because I'd lose my determination if I let him say anything that would distract me from an apology. "I never told you why I broke up with you."

A strange look passed over Lucas's face. "No. You didn't."

"That letter. The one my dad sent me? I got it the day... the day I broke things off. Seeing his letter, it was a huge reminder that he left me. Not that I could ever really forget it, but it was like a slap in the face." I swallowed hard, my face starting to warm. I had to keep going. "It got me thinking about the night before, when we almost—well, it made me think about if it was so easy for my dad to walk away, it'd be that much easier for you to leave too. And I panicked."

More like I'd self-destructed. Instead of talking to Lucas about it, instead of talking to *anyone* about it, I'd started burning bridges. Struck a match and lit everything on fire.

I looked down at myself, at the way the dark hemline pooled onto the grass. "I'm so sorry for not telling you the truth. I'm sorry you got dragged in the middle of everything."

Breathe, Blaire, I tried to tell myself, but I couldn't. It was impossible when I knew Lucas stood there, saying *nothing*. I could hear his steady breathing, see his shoes from the corner of my eye, but no words came out of his mouth.

Until— "You didn't break up with me because you don't love me anymore?" The words were barely above a whisper. "You were afraid I'd leave you?"

I made a face at the ground. "Maybe I broke up with you because you're a bad listener."

"Blaire Beverly," he said. The expression on Lucas's face was nothing short of *soft*. I couldn't describe the way he looked at me, like I was some sort of precious jewel that'd been offered out to him. He dipped his head. "Do you seriously think I'd just give up on us without an explanation? That I'd leave you all alone?"

I held his gaze, trying to be like him and scan the depths of his soul, but I could never see deeper than the surface. I always got too lost in the color. "My dad did. Why couldn't you?"

"Why do you think I've stuck around all this time? Even after you dumped me, I was there. Even when you didn't want me to be, even when you straight-up ignored me. I love you. I'm not going to *walk away*."

For some reason, that only made everything worse. "We're in *high school*, Lucas. What if you only *think* you love me because you don't know any better?"

Lucas reached out and pulled one of my hands into his, touch gentle enough to draw goosebumps, much more potent than the shivers of the night breeze. "As much as I know it right now, I know that I love you."

No idea where all the oxygen had gone, because suddenly, I couldn't breathe. Hearing him say those things now made something turn over inside me, like a deadbolt on a door flipping open. I imagined slapping my hand over it, trying to flip it back, but it was no use.

And I wanted nothing more to return the smile, to dissolve into his embrace like I had so many times before.

But something in me held back. "I'm snarky and

dramatic and shove things down and do the wrong thing. A lot. I hurt you. How can you just forgive me?"

"I want this, Bee." Lucas's expression filled with hope and tenderness, one that could've made me start to cry again. "I want to be there for you. Watch scary movies and video-chat with you later when I'm afraid of the shadows. To help with the catering and kiss you on my couch. I'm here. I'm not going anywhere, not anytime soon. I'm all yours." He added, "If you still want me."

Each one of his words settled inside me, like little stones settling at the bottom of a stream. He was Lucas, beautiful Lucas, offering his heart to me even though I'd crushed it before. With his dark hair and stunning blue eyes, curling smile and gentle touch.

"I'm no princess," I whispered to him, trembling, staring at the spot where our fingers joined. With my free hand, I grabbed the black material of my dress, lifting so the hem pulled from the ground. "But the shoes do sort of fit."

Lucas's gaze dropped as I lifted the bottom of the dress to reveal the horrible, tiny, ugly plastic shoes I'd shoved my feet into. They felt two sizes too small, like they always had, but now I found myself not hating them as much. I thought of all the times I'd given Gram crap for these shoes, and now they came in handy.

My princess shoes glittered in the dull light, looking almost like actual glass slippers.

Lucas looked at them for a long moment, as if the shoes themselves were a spell that held his gaze. I held my breath as the moment of quiet expanded, hoping he understood, my heart about to burst.

And, ever so slowly, he looked up, at me. "They don't really match your witchy getup, Bee."

A startled laugh burst from me. "This is me trying to say I'll be the sort-of princess to your prince. You're supposed to be a couple at this party thing, right?"

The grin on Lucas's face lit up my insides, realization dawning. It was his real smile, his brilliant teeth showing, the dimple in his bottom lip coming out, the indentation on the left corner of his mouth pushed in. He reached out and pulled one of my hands away from my dress, linking his fingers through mine.

"I'm not perfect," I rushed to say. "I screwed up, pushing you away when I should've kept you close. And I'm sorry. I promise next time I won't run." The words flowed from me in an effortless sort of stream, and I couldn't understand why I'd been so nervous before. Being here with him, with our fingers entwined, I'd never felt more at ease. More at home. "Thank you for sticking by me even though I was a pain. And for getting me coffee."

"Donnie told you about that, huh?" He chuckled. "It was purely selfish, I promise. I couldn't let you go."

And thank goodness for that.

I reached up and traced my fingertips along the sharpness of his jaw, back until my hand rested on the side of his neck. "I love you," I told him, the emotion blooming in my chest, unraveling my sanity. "No one knows the future, but I know I want to face it with you."

"That—" Lucas's voice lowered to a whisper as he placed a hand on my waist and pulled me close, "—was tremendously cheesy. I mean it. I cringed a little."

I shook my head back and forth, and I told him, "Just shut up and kiss me."

No hesitation. Lucas leaned forward in one swift movement and pressed his lips against mine.

For a moment, the warmth of his mouth shocked me, the way it always used to at first. His lips kissed the cold from mine, responding almost like no time had passed. Heat flooded through me, wiping any trace of my goosebumps. Gosh, it'd been so long since our last kiss. Too long. My head spun with the taste of him, familiar and tender and rich. It turned deeper when I parted my lips beneath his, pulling him closer, closer, until not a sliver of space existed between us.

People still laughed and teased and danced around us, but in that moment, it was just him and me.

I pressed closer, dropping the broom so I could wrap my arms around his neck. It clattered against the ground, but it barely registered.

How I'd lived without this, I had no idea, but I did know I never wanted to do it again. And it'd be different. For me, there was no more running. I wasn't going to push away those who meant the most to me. I wasn't going to isolate myself anymore.

Surrounded by Halloween decorations and people in wild costumes, I relaxed in Lucas's arms, finally knowing things would be all right.

epilogue

I pulled the pen up from the paper with a sharp breath, looking at the page filled with looping black letters, scrawled by a nervous hand. At the bottom, my scribbled signature was illegible, but the two B's were clear. Blaire Beverly.

And at the top, two daunting words. *Dear Dad.*

I never thought I'd write those words. Especially not in this past month since receiving his letter. I honestly hadn't thought I'd get to this point. Forgiveness had been elusive, intangible, but here I was. The piece of stationary overflowed with lines poured from my heart, filling the page. And looking it over, it finally felt *right*.

"Blaire, Aimee called up and said Lucas and Donnie are downstairs," Gram said as she stepped into the doorway of my bedroom, eyes immediately drawing over to where I sat at my desk. And then to the paper in front of me. "How's draft number three going?"

I reached out and traced my signature. "I think it needs

one more revision. I finally figured out how to say everything, but it could be polished a bit better."

The floorboards creaked as Gram stepped further into my room, coming to rest her hand on my shoulder. "Do you mind if I stick mine in with yours when you send it?"

Gram had written a letter of her own to Dad, but neither of us had told the other of the contents. She'd written about her personal feelings and I'd written about mine, and only Dad would get to know them. We'd made that decision after I'd let Gram read the first draft of my letter, and she hadn't been sure if I should've called Dad a butt—or, you know, a not-so-polite synonym for butt.

"Sounds perfect to me," I said, pushing to my feet to wrap my arms around her. She was so much shorter than me, so much daintier, and I couldn't help but smile. "I'll see you tonight."

Gram gave me a squeeze before she released me. "Have fun. Tell Lucas again how much I appreciated his help cleaning up Saturday night, will you?"

Lucas had stayed late after the Bash a week ago, cleaning up the booth with us—and then cleaning up the disaster area of a kitchen we'd left at the shop. He'd had no problem stepping back into his role as a helper at Costume Catering, hauling things back and forth, and even lending a hand to Aunt Aimee to wash dishes. It wasn't the way I'd wanted us to spend our first night together as a couple again—it would've involved much more alone time—but it was still good to see him around my family.

It was good to have him around.

"I will," I promised her, and headed out.

Aunt Aimee sat at the front counter of the shop with a large planner opened in front of her, murmuring slightly under her breath.

"Planning our next outing?" I asked as I came out of the stairwell. "Any more costume parties?"

"Those are dying off." She tapped her pen against a blank section of the planner. "We're going into the holiday season, so everyone's going to want us to wear our normal catering uniforms. Make sure your black pants fit, okay?"

"As soon as I get back, I'll try them on." I glanced around the room. "The boys are—"

"Outside." Aunt Aimee shook her head with a fond smile. "How you managed to convince Donnie to go on a walk, I have no clue. I'm never able to convince him to go with John and me."

I patted her on the shoulder before walking around the side of the desk. "That's because he'd rather walk with his cool friends than his lame parents."

Aunt Aimee gave a loud gasp, but I slipped safely out of reach when she tried to reach out and smack me.

The door chimed and I hauled it opened and hurried outside, not putting it past Aunt Aimee to throw her pen in my direction. I could feel my smile, wide on my face, as I stepped out onto the sidewalk, and it only deepened when I turned and saw two figures leaning up against the building.

Donnie leaned against the shop's wall, blue coffee cup in his hand, but straightened when he saw me. "Huh. I didn't realize how long it's been since I've seen you smile like that."

"I'm in a pretty good mood," I told him, my gaze shifting to the boy to his right

Looking at Lucas gave my heart race, even though it hadn't even been a full day since I'd seen him. No, I'd seen him last night, when we'd taken Delia to the movie theater over in Bayview. He wore the black jacket he always wore, even though soon he'd have to break out a warmer coat. Cooler temperatures descended fast, but even slightly underdressed, he still was stunningly handsome, enough to make my brain hurt.

He still was propped up against the brick building, both hands holding the signature Crushed Beanz coffee cups, looking at me with an expression so warm it could've chased the cold air away.

I didn't even realize we'd stood there, staring at each other, until Donnie groaned. "You know, I was starting to get used to you two not making me gag all the time. Seriously."

"You're ridiculous," I said with a roll of my eyes, but my cheeks heated.

"Here's your espresso," Lucas said as he passed one cup to me. "Just as you like it."

The cup instantly warmed my hands as I latched on. "Thanks. Can we walk through Kepler park on the edge of town? Those trees always have the prettiest colors."

Donnie grumbled an affirmative and turned on his heel, leaving Lucas and me to follow. Immediately, Lucas held his free hand out to me. When I took it, he didn't lace our fingers together—no, he pulled me quickly forward, giving my body no choice but to fall against him, not an inch between us. I'd barely had any time to tilt my coffee so it wouldn't spill.

"Hurry," Lucas mock-whispered. "Kiss me while he's not looking."

"You're ridiculous," I scoffed, but pushed onto my tiptoes anyway.

Denying a boy as beautiful as Lucas when he requested a kiss was insanity. I couldn't do it. His mouth heated my own, like sun melting snow. I could taste the macchiato on his lips, and my chest, my blood, my brain—all of me felt *warm*.

After stealing one more kiss, I leaned back. "I love you," he whispered against my skin.

I opened my mouth to say it back when Donnie cut over me, voice loud. "You have got to be *kidding me*. Do I need to separate you two?"

I couldn't fight the grin that surfaced as Donnie glared between the two of us.

"We're coming," Lucas assured him with a slight chuckle, drawing away and grabbing my hand. "Right behind you."

"It's what you're *doing* right behind me that freaks me out."

I cuddled closer to the boy at my side as we walked along the sidewalk, loving how he pulled me firmer against him, how he leaned down to kiss the top of my head. "I love you too," I whispered back, hooking my fingers in his belt loops and hanging on tight.

Donnie started to talk to Lucas about school, and I sipped at my espresso, glancing between them as the bitterness stole over my tongue. Donnie, with his spiked hair poking out from underneath his cap. Lucas, with his content half-smile on his face while the two spoke, blue eyes periodically drifting down to me.

I'd almost given all of this up. All of this. I huddled deeper against Lucas's side, vowing I'd never make that mistake ever again.

TWO KINDS OF US

Two Kinds of Us

Diamonds meet rock n' roll and secrets meet their end.

CHRISTMAS AS WE KNOW IT

Christmas As We Know It

Meet me underneath the mistletoe.

TEACHING THE TEACHER'S PET

Teaching the Teacher's Pet

Tutoring sessions in both algebra and love...which one will get schooled?

DREAMING ABOUT THE BOY NEXT DOOR

Dreaming About the Boy Next Door

Kissing your best friend's brother is never a good idea, but I went ahead and did it anyway.

Order your copy today!

Acknowledgements

My fingers are trembling as I type this. This little page is just as surreal as the rest of the story. I cannot believe we made it to this moment.

I truly couldn't have done it with my army behind me. My fantastic beta readers read this baby from ground zero, when she wasn't too pretty and hugely bratty. I think we all know, dear betas, how cringey that first draft was, and I thank you for putting up with it! Those betas specially—Ashley, Angie, Cassie, Valerie, Steph, and Stacey!

Thank you to my critique partner, Ariel. You always listen when I come at you with book-related questions. I struggled with figuring Blaire out at first, but you coached me through it!

My dear parents—thank you for putting up with my anxiousness revolving around this story. Dad, I can still remember you telling me "Are you seriously turning into that person? What happened to the girl who loved writing?" I'm here, Dad. Thank you for reminding me. And Mom, thank you for listening to my babble about these characters. Even though you might not have been able to sort through the threads of my brain every time, you always listened and let me talk it out, and that means more than you could know!

And, finally, thank You for giving me this passion and desire. Thank You for directing my steps and leading me on this path. This idea was planted into my head by You, and I can never thank You enough.

Made in United States
North Haven, CT
21 April 2023